THE DRAGON EXPERIMENT

A Here Be Dragons Novel

LOUISA MASTERS

The Dragon Experiment

THE DRAGON EXPERIMENT

Who knew sleeping around could save the entire species?

I'm a simple dragon. Give me knowledge, give me research, give me rings for my hoard, and give me athletic men who want to get sweaty between the sheets… or anywhere else. Those things make me happy. Other things… well, who cares about those?

Turns out, I should have cared. Or at least paid attention. Because I somehow signed up for a scientific study run by a shy, nerdy sorcerer with the body of a god. And the study just happens to be about my favorite form of exercise.

It doesn't take long for me to know I want to do more than science with Rhys. Although I've never been the kind of dragon to mix feelings with fun, Rhys could be the one person who meets all my needs, even if he won't wear a ring on every finger.

But when his research becomes more important than any of us could have imagined, our relationship enters a new phase. Now it's up to me to show Rhys how much he's worth… both to me and to the future of his species.

FOUR YEARS AGO

I DON'T KNOW why I thought this was a good idea. It seemed clever at the time, using a stand in the mall concourse to attract people to my study, but in reality, it's been a waste of time. Although I have made a profit from selling rings to humans.

Ordinary rings, of course, not the special ones for the study. They look the same, but there's no way I'd give a human a ring imbued with sorcery. My biggest mistake, though, was the rings themselves. I got a great deal on a bulk lot from a distributor going out of business. The rep I spoke to told me they were engraved with "purity," but I figured that wouldn't matter. It's just a word, right?

Wrong. Turns out, humans take this shit seriously. The distributor sent pamphlets and everything. Humans are polarized by purity rings, either flocking to me or avoiding me completely. And community members are steering clear, which is damn annoying since they're the people I need. I've only managed to sign three people up to my study this whole week, when I was hoping for ten times that.

A good-looking guy with dark hair wanders over, his gaze glued to the display case. "Look at the pretties," he breathes.

"Hi," I greet, squinting at him slightly. There's something about him… he's not part of the community, but he's definitely not human either. He must be either an elf or a dragon, which is both shocking and super cool. I've been too busy with my research to pay attention to most things happening in the world, but not even I could miss the news that a year ago, elves and dragons from another dimension migrated to Earth to avoid extinction.

This is *amazing*! It would be incredible to have one of them as part of my study.

Clearing my throat in an attempt to rein in my excitement, I check first that he's not just a human with weird energy. "You moved here not long ago, right? With your *family*? At the invitation of our mutual acquaintance, Percy?"

He tears his gaze away from the shiny silver and gold rings in the case long enough to nod. "Yes. I'm Fabian Draco. You're part of the community?" He studies me. "Sorcerer, right?"

Yes! "Right," I agree. *Be calm and professional.* Draco, that means dragon. "I wonder if you'd be interested in participating in a research study I'm running on the effects of sex on metaphysical health?"

His attention is back on the case. "Sure," he says absently.

Grinning, I grab the paperwork explaining the study,

but before I can start talking him through it, three human teenagers come over to peer into the case, whispering to each other. Holding back a sigh, I begin my fake spiel instead. I can't let them overhear anything that might give away our existence.

"Are you pure of heart, sir?"

He looks up, surprise on his face, and I flick my gaze sideways toward the teens, hoping he'll get the hint. "Of course I am," he says, and I smile in relief.

"Wonderful! And are you committed to your purity and willing to wear a symbol of it for all to see and know?"

The girls exchange glances and back away, hurrying off quickly. Thank fuck.

"Is the symbol one of these rings?" Fabian Draco asks, pointing into the case.

"Yeah. Sorry about that. I didn't want those girls to hear anything they shouldn't."

He nods seriously. "Secrecy is important. Could I try on that silver one there?"

Wow, he's into this. "Sure." I pull out the ring he indicated to and hand it to him, noticing that he's already wearing three rings on each hand. "Let me walk you through the study. It's pretty simple. I'm researching how sex can impact the health of magic or power in different species. Humans have done studies to show that sex affects physical and mental health, but of course they can't research things like sorcery ability or vampire charisma. My hypothesis is that regular healthy sex will improve each species' innate ability."

Fabian nods, his eyes on the ring.

"There's a sorcery weave on the ring that will bond to your body and send me information. On a daily basis, it will be things like your heart rate, blood pressure, and general level of health—the kind of things humans determine with a basic exam and blood test—as well as an energy reading of your innate magical ability. When you have sex, it will send me that same information again. That will allow me to track the impact of sex on your body and magic both while you're having it, within the twenty-four hours after, and on an ongoing basis."

He slides the ring onto his finger and tilts his hand to catch the light. "It's a bit snug," he comments.

"I can get you a bigger size if you want, but since you'll be wearing it all the time anyway, snug isn't a huge issue. You don't want it to fall off." I chuckle, then I hurry to explain why. "It can't fall off. Not unless you stop having sex. The bond will keep it in place as long as you're sexually active. If you stop having sex for three months, the bond will deactivate and the ring will come off. If you want to stop participating in the study while you're still sexually active, just come and see me and I'll take the ring off." Is he even listening? He seems to have zoned out, all his attention on the ring. That's not good —I can't sign him up to this study without informed consent.

"Fabian, do you understand what I've explained?"

He blinks at me. "Of course. If I don't want the ring anymore, I bring it back to you."

"Let's go through the paperwork," I suggest. "This is basically what I've just told you but with more technical details. I need your signature, and I'll give you a copy to take with you in case you want to refer back to it."

"Do you have a pen so I can sign it?" he asks, and it's my turn to blink.

"You don't want to read through it all?"

Shrugging, he says, "If it's just the same information you've told me, I don't need to." His gaze goes back to the glint of the silver ring.

Somewhat reluctantly, I hand him a pen. If I wasn't so desperate for participants, I'd probably refuse him. He seems just a bit vague. But it's not like the study is invasive or dangerous, and if he changes his mind, it's a simple thing for me to release the sorcery weave that will bond the ring to him.

He signs and dates the papers, then reaches into his pocket. "How much?"

"Uh, no, there's no cost to you," I assure him. "All costs have been covered already."

"Great!" He grins broadly. "Thank you!"

"Wait!" Hurriedly, I focus on the ring and activate the weaves in it, bringing the sorcery that will bond with him to life. I give it a metaphysical ID code and hastily note that down on my copy of his consent form. "Here, this is yours." I staple my business card to his copy and hold it out to him. "Feel free to call me if you have any questions."

"I think it should be fine, but thanks." He takes the papers, waves, and disappears into the crowd.

That did not go how I thought it would.

CHAPTER ONE

Fabian

I FOLLOW Brandt and Percy out of the kitchen and down the hall to one of the little parlors. This one has beautiful windows and a small piano, which means we usually refer to it as the music room.

Percy waves me over to the sofa and closes the door behind me. He's frowning—he really thought ice and butter would get my ring off, and he kept saying "I don't understand why it's stuck. Your finger isn't swollen."

I don't really understand why the ring has to come off at all. It's pretty and looks good on me. Sure, it's been stuck on my hand for four years, and it says "purity," which, when I bought it, I didn't realize meant something different to humans than it does to me, but who really cares? Brandt and Percy are determined, though, and it might be nice to be able to wear a different ring on that finger. I have a very nice one in silver and gold that looks like two snakes twined together.

So I sit next to Brandt on the sofa and hold out my hand when he gestures. He studies it carefully, and then

I feel the warm flow of his magic probing. I could have done this myself, but Brandt's magic *is* stronger than mine.

"Huh."

"Huh, what?" Percy asks anxiously, hovering beside us. "Is it infected or something?"

"No," I say. "I'd know if it was infected." Wouldn't I? Infected with what? "What kind of infection?"

They ignore me. "No, it's not infected," Brandt says slowly, frowning. "It's not coming off, however. There's some kind of… I think the ring was ensorcelled?"

"Really?"

"What?"

Percy and I speak in unison. "Why would someone have done that to my pretty ring?" I demand. "Is it damaged?"

The look Percy gives me is patient and long-suffering. "More importantly, what are the weaves doing?"

Brandt shakes his head slowly. "I can't tell. Dragon magic and sorcery are too different. It might even be elf magic, although I don't think so."

Unable to resist, I test the ring with my own magic. Surely I would know if I'd been wearing sorcery on my hand for the last f— Oh yeah, there *is* something there. Huh. I wonder how I never noticed?

"…not harmful?" Percy asks. "I know it's been there for years, but I'd hate for it to be something dormant that activates because we didn't move fast enough."

"Like what?" I ask curiously. "Is there a tradition of ensorcelled jewelry that activates after the owner is lulled into complacency? Are there records? I'd like to see the history." I hesitate. "Don't tell Steffen."

They both widen their eyes. "Steffen can never learn of this," Brandt orders vehemently.

"Never," Percy adds. "He'd take all your rings. And everyone else's."

I nod emphatically. "It stays between us." Steffen is a good friend and an average roommate, but he's also paranoid about our security. If he found out I'm wearing an ensorcelled ring that does something we don't know about, he'd be unbearable. I wouldn't put it past him to go through all our stuff and quarantine or destroy anything he considered unsafe. "But what do I do now?"

Brandt makes a face. "I don't think it's dangerous, but I wouldn't stake your life on that. And since I can't tell what it's supposed to do, I guess the best thing would be to have a sorcerer take a look."

"I'll call David," Percy offers, referring to his friend who's a sorcerer. "We can fly out to see him this afternoon."

I try not to whine as I say, "Does it have to be today? I'm kinda tired." My hookup last night wore me out. In the best way, of course. Which reminds me, I need a shower. He was a messy fuck.

Percy and Brandt do that wordless communication thing couples sometimes do. It intrigues and annoys me. I don't like being left out of a conversation, but I do admire superpowers and want to know exactly how it works.

"I guess it can wait until tomorrow," Percy concedes reluctantly.

"Or Tuesday? Because I have a class I can't miss tomorrow." So far, I'm really loving this whole college thing. My scope for hookups has widened a *lot*. It seems there are a lot of "straight" college guys who are open to new experiences but not bold enough to use Grindr or visit a gay club. I've only been a student for a few weeks, but already I've learned new things. And not just in class.

Percy doesn't look happy about it, but he agrees.

"Great! Now, will someone explain to me what's going on with Dustin and his professor?" I got home from my night out in time for lunch, only to discover that the professor Dustin's been crushing on for two years was joining us. I thought that meant Dustin had finally made a move on him, but instead I got this jumbled explanation about how they weren't going to have sex.

"They're going to discuss how they want their relationship to progress," Brandt says calmly. "Rob feels that because Dustin used to be his student, there are some boundaries he needs to respect."

Yeah, that makes no sense. I'll ask Dustin later. "So can I teach a course on dragon culture?" That's the other thing that got mentioned during lunch, and I *love* the idea. As the official historian and record keeper for dragonkind, I know almost everything there is to know about us, and what little I don't know, I have access to. The living archive is merely a thought away.

"I think it's a great idea," Brandt affirms. "People here are mostly used to us, but there are still times they have questions."

We both look at Percy, who's smiling faintly.

"Yes. But I'd like to see what you plan to talk about before we start spreading the word. There are some things people just aren't ready to know about dragons."

I'm not sure what he could possibly mean, since

we're just plain awesome, but I trust Percy to know what's right for us. Brandt's been a wonderful wing leader for a long time, but one of the best things he ever did was hook up with Percy.

"No problem," I promise, then leave them to canoodle while I go have a shower, admire my hoard of pretty rings, and think about all the dragonish things I can teach others.

ON TUESDAY MORNING, I obediently fly into the city so Percy can take me to have my ring examined. Thankfully, he gives me coffee and a pastry when I arrive. Kethe cooked the usual full breakfast before I left, but flying is hungry work.

The building that houses the offices of the Dragon Elf Alliance government is nice enough, as far as office buildings go. Percy's old stomping grounds, the Community of Species Government offices, are in the same building, which is why he's brought me here. Technically, as the guardian of all dragon history and knowledge, I guess I should be working here too, but I don't do well in such a structured environment. Before we found our country estate, Here Be Dragons, I had a space in these offices, and I never got any work done. I function much better with my own quiet room at home, and Brandt knows it. It's easy enough for me to come in here if I need to.

For now, though, I dutifully follow Percy and Brandt into the building, winking at the security guard I hooked up with right after we came to Earth. He was lovely—so energetic and perfectly amenable to a few quick fucks in the security office without wanting anything more. There's nothing worse than a hookup who doesn't want to say goodbye. I have fond memories of the guard, even if I can't quite remember his name.

Percy and I get off the elevator at the CSG floor, while Brandt goes directly to his office at the DEA. "David will see you first thing," Percy says, "so we can have the rest of the day, if necessary, to work out what's needed to get the ring off."

"Okay," I agree amiably, still not really sure why it's such a big deal. I mean, yeah, it would be nice to be able to take the ring off and wear something different sometimes, and I definitely would prefer if my pretty didn't turn out to be a dormant murder ring, but it wouldn't be the end of the world if I had to keep it on. Its elegant simplicity suits my fingers.

Maybe this is one of those things everyone else seems to know but I just don't get.

We see David before we get to his office. He's standing in the hallway, talking to someone I don't recognize, and I take a moment to admire him. With his black hair and blue eyes and classic features, he really is very nice to look at. Alas, looking is all I can do—he was snatched up by Caolan, an elf who works with Brandt sometimes, before I ever even got to Earth. I once asked Caolan if they were looking for an occasional third, and he told me in no uncertain terms that he wasn't sharing David, then went on a rant about dragons trying to steal his boyfriend. I've got no idea what brought that on.

David sees us, smiles at his companion and excuses himself, then comes down the hall to meet us halfway. "Good morning. Fabian, it's good to see you again. I've booked a meeting room for us so we can have some privacy." He and Percy lead the way, and I take the opportunity to admire his ass. Caolan really is a lucky elf.

The meeting room we go into is small, the four-seat table almost filling it, but it will serve its purpose. I make myself comfortable in one of the chairs while David closes the door.

"Okay," he says, joining us, "let me see your ring."

I hold out my hand, and Percy sighs. "The other ring, Fabian."

Ohhhh. I suppose that makes sense. "Sorry," I say, swapping hands. "I thought this one"—I wave the hand bearing the chunky platinum ring studded with pieces of aquamarine—"was more your style."

David's smile is kind and patient. "It is, but let's take care of this little problem first. Then you can show me the rest."

He's such a nice man. Caolan's nice too, so I guess them hooking up makes sense.

David studies my not-really purity ring with a frown on his handsome face. "Well, the good news is, it's not dangerous."

"Are you sure?" Percy asks anxiously, then adds, "Sorry. Of course you're sure."

"I'm positive. This won't harm you at all. It's a monitoring weave, and it looks like it's coded for health."

I frown. Something about that sounds familiar. "Like, it makes me more healthy?"

David shakes his head. "No. It's checking your baseline health and reporting back to the sorcerer who wove it. There's something else here too—special reports at certain times. I'm not familiar enough with this type of weave to tell when without examining it more closely."

"Someone's spying on Fabian?" Percy sounds shocked. "Why?"

"Because I'm good-looking and interesting?" I try not to be offended that he needed to ask.

"Of course," he soothes. "But someone who recognizes that wouldn't just be spying on your baseline health. They'd want to know what you're doing and saying, and the ring doesn't track that… does it?"

"Nope," David confirms. "It's not overtly spying in any way. This is pretty much what a healer would give you to run tests over several days or weeks. Like if you had a cardiac condition and they wanted to monitor your heart. I can't think why a stalker would want this kind of information."

"So why won't it come off?" I ask curiously.

He tips my hand, studying the ring from a different angle, and I admire the way it gleams in the light. So pretty. "That part of the weave is linked to those special reports. This really isn't my specialty, but the more I look at it, the more I think it might be a medical monitoring device. Where did you get it, again?"

"At the mall. There was a guy selling them in the concourse. I didn't realize until a few days later that it's supposed to be a purity ring." I roll my eyes. That's still something I struggle to understand. I can respect people not having sex because they don't want to, but to tie sex, a basic bodily function, to "purity" just seems bizarre to me.

David frowns. "A sorcerer was selling human religious items?"

I open my mouth to respond and then close it again. I hadn't thought of it that way. "He was a sorcerer," I say slowly, "and he sold me the ring. I remember him asking if I was pure of heart. But mostly he seemed not to care about religion? He talked about the ring for a while and made me sign a form."

David starts to chuckle, and Percy closes his eyes and sighs.

"What?"

"Is it at all possible that you signed up for a medical study or trial?" David asks.

I blink. "Wouldn't he have told me that?"

"Yes. When he was talking about the ring, what did he say?"

I shrug. "Something about how if I didn't want the ring anymore, I needed to bring it back to him."

They exchange glances. "So it's possible he was talking about you not wanting to participate in the trial anymore? What about the form you had to sign? Did he give you a copy?"

"Yes!" He did! I remember that.

"Great!" Percy grins in relief. "So we can check that for the details. It would probably have the sorcerer's contact information too, right?"

"Definitely." David nods.

Er… "I don't think I have it anymore?"

Percy sighs again. "Why not?"

I spread my hands. "I didn't think I'd ever need to get in touch with him. I mean, why would I want to give back my ring?" I wriggle my fingers to show it off.

David snorts. "Because it's actually a monitoring device in an experimental trial you know nothing about?"

Horror slaps me. "The weave doesn't hurt the ring, does it?" I lift my hand and hold the ring so close to my face, my eyes cross, trying to see if my poor baby has been damaged in any way.

"No, the weave doesn't hurt the ring." David's patient tone seems a little less patient. "The ring is fine. Let me have another look at it so I can grab a signature off the weave, and then I'll ask around and see who's doing research that might need something like this."

Reluctantly, I hold out my hand again. "I'm not giving the ring back," I warn. "So if you think that might happen, don't waste your time asking."

"They won't take it back, Fabian. You paid for it." Percy sounds like he wants to sigh again. I don't understand why everyone is so huffy today.

"No, it was free."

They exchange looks again.

"Well, that gives more weight to the assumption it's a trial," David says. "But weren't you suspicious that a sorcerer was supposedly selling religious jewelry and then gave it to you for free after making you sign a consent form?"

I shrug. "Why would I be?"

"Why indeed," Percy murmurs.

CHAPTER TWO

Rhys

I'M deep in analyzing last month's data when a hand lands on my shoulder and scares the living daylights out of me.

After shrieking in terror and prying myself off the ceiling, I wait for Sura, one of my colleagues here at the lab and probably my closest friend—ex-friend if she doesn't stop laughing—to get her breath back.

"Sorry," she gasps. "I didn't mean to startle you. I forgot how focused you get."

Suuuuure she did. It's not like we haven't been friends for sixty years or anything. Not like we haven't worked in the same lab for half that time. Not like she doesn't do this to me every few weeks.

I fold my arms across my chest and quirk a brow.

"Whew," she says finally, wiping a tear of laughter from the corner of her eye. "Um. The front desk got an inquiry that I think might be about your research."

My heartbeat picks up a fraction. "My research? From who?" I've always hoped to attract attention from a high-profile patron or investor who could get me the money I need to expand my study. But the trials I'm doing aren't interesting enough. One investor I approached told me that while sex sells, my research is not sexy enough. He suggested I require that the sexual interactions of my participants be "more heavily monitored" and followed that up with a wink. It took me a few seconds to understand that he was talking about video, and then I told him to keep his money and left.

Sura shrugs. "I didn't see. The receptionists were talking about it and trying to figure out who to send it to. Something about a ring that monitors baseline health. That's yours, right?"

She knows it is. "I guess I'll go find out." It seems unlikely a patron would have that much information but not my name, but who knows what rich people talk about at cocktail parties. Maybe they heard some of the details but not all of them.

She starts chuckling again as I leave the lab, and I know she's thinking about how high I jumped. I can't help it if I block out the world when I concentrate.

Our current receptionists are Taryn and Chris. We turn over support staff a lot here at Kendall Research and Development, because some of us (not me) are doing research that makes loud noises and knocks down walls. After one of my colleagues lost track of a little weave she called her mobile firebug, and said firebug wandered out of the fireproof lab into the rest of the building and—you guessed it—set fire to lots of things, the staff have been especially jumpy. That was a few months ago now, and I've heard them muttering that a new catastrophe must be on the way soon. I suppose I can't blame them for being nervous, but things like this happen when you work in research.

They look up warily as I approach the desk. Mostly they like me, since my research never created a sonic boom that caused them to lose their hearing for a day, but they still regard all of us who work in the labs with healthy distrust.

"Hi," I greet cheerfully. It's fake cheer, of course. I'm never this happy about talking to people I don't know that well. "I heard you've had an inquiry about rings that monitor baseline health?"

"Oh!" Taryn sounds surprised. "Yes. Is that yours?" She grabs a pile of message notes and leafs through them.

"I think so. I'm definitely using rings to monitor baseline health in my study's participants."

She hands over the note. "He seemed keen for someone to call him back."

"Thanks, Taryn. I'll take care of it." I give them both a smile and an awkward little wave, then walk back toward my lab while reading the message.

Looking for researcher using purity rings to monitor baseline health. Study at least 4 years old. Please call David Carew.

There's a phone number at the bottom, but my gaze is stuck on the name. David Carew? Surely not the same David Carew who's the lucifer's right hand? My study isn't the kind of research the government usually takes an interest in. Maybe once I've conclusively proved the connection between sex and improved metaphysical health, I'll be able to get some buy-in—after all, governments like cheap, easy ways to keep citizens healthy—but while I'm still gathering data, it's unlikely they'll want to know about it.

No, this is probably someone else with the same name.

Regardless, curiosity is eating at me now. Whoever this is, the fact that he knows I used "purity" rings means he's had contact with one of my participants, so it's odd that he doesn't have my name.

Bypassing the lab, I go into the shoebox office I share with my labmates. There are four of us, all doing low-risk research. Which often means low profit and is why we get such a poky office. We spend most of our time in the lab anyway, so it's not a big deal, and the office being empty now means I can make this call in peace.

The phone rings three times before someone answers. "CSG executive reception, this is Candice."

My stomach drops, and for a moment I forget how to speak.

"Hello?" the sweet voice says.

"Uh, yes, hello. Sorry. I got, um, I was distracted. Could I speak with David Carew, please?" Who is actually the David Carew helping the lucifer run our government.

"Let me see if David's available. Who shall I say is calling?"

"Rhys Griffiths. Dr. Griffiths. From Kendall R&D. Um, I'm returning his call. About—" I make myself stop. The receptionist doesn't need to hear my word vomit.

"Thank you, Dr. Griffiths. I'll just be a moment."

As I listen to soothing instrumental hold music, I pinch myself. It hurts. I guess that means I'm awake? But why on earth would David Carew from CSG be calling about my research?

Oh *fuck*, what if that asshole who thought I could make my study more interesting by turning it into porn has been shooting his mouth and somehow the government thinks I'm making sex tapes under the guise of legitimate research?

But... wouldn't I just get a visit from enforcement if that was the case?

"Dr. Griffiths, this is David Carew," a smooth, pleasant voice says in my ear, yanking me out of my weird thoughts and causing me to squeak. I really hope he didn't hear that. "Thanks for calling me back."

"No pleasure." I close my eyes and wonder what I did in a past life to deserve this. "I mean, it's no problem. My pleasure."

He hesitates, and when he speaks again, there's the faintest note of amusement there. "Are you conducting research through the use of purity rings that monitor baseline health?"

"Yes, I am. I hope you don't mind me asking, but where did you hear about my study? I didn't think it was something that would interest CSG just yet."

"I'm not sure that it would. I don't actually know any more about your study than what I've said. I was trying to find you on behalf of a friend."

That clears up nothing.

"Oh?"

"Yes. Four years ago, he signed up for your study without realizing it."

"I always explain the study in detail," I protest hotly. I *will not* be accused of unethical behavior. "Also, everyone signs a consent form and is given a copy."

"No, I don't doubt that. My friend can be... uh, somewhat vague. The way I understand it, he was enamored by the ring and didn't pay close attention to what you were saying."

The uneasy feeling in my stomach multiplies. I can only remember one participant who seemed zoned out when I signed him up, and he's the source of my most valuable data. If he wants to back out now, I'll cry. While the study is set up so I don't usually know which participant is the source of which data, for the first few years I only had one dragon participant, and his baseline is different enough from the other participants that I could tell what data was his.

Or… what if he decides he doesn't want to be part of the study at all and asks me to destroy all his data? I'm not legally obligated to do so—he did sign the consent form of his own free will after I explained the study to him—but I would feel morally that I should. That would decimate my research. So many of the tacks I've taken the last few years have been based on his data. Nobody else who signed up has sex so often or so many times in one session. At first I thought it might be a dragon thing, but about a year and a half ago, I managed to sign up two other dragons, and neither of them are anywhere close.

Swallowing hard, I make myself say, "For privacy reasons, I can't confirm or deny anyone's participation in the study. But if your friend wants to drop out of the program, I'll give you my direct number for them to call, and we'll set up an exit interview."

"I don't know if he'll want to drop out or not. Especially if that would mean giving back the ring." He chuckles. "Could you tell me more about the study, please?"

"Uh, sure. Of course. My hypothesis is that regular satisfying sex can improve metaphysical health in the same way it improves physical and mental health." I explain the details of the study and how the rings and monitoring play into it, emphasizing that the monitoring only tells me baseline health and metaphysical health information. I don't need anyone thinking I'm spying on their sex partners.

"That's fascinating," David says when I'm done, and he genuinely sounds interested. "What are your results like so far?"

"Excellent." I can't hide how smug I am. "I'm nearly five years in, and all the trends show that frequent, healthy sex results in better metaphysical health. That includes masturbation," I tack on. "I'll be publishing interim results within the year and then moving into phase two of the study. I anticipate publishing the final results within the next five years." I could do it sooner, but I need more participants and thus more money. As it is, if someone comes along with research the board of KRD really wants to back, I might have some of my funding cut. The perils of not being "sexy" enough.

There's a pause, and I wonder if the line's dropped out. "Hello? Are you still there?"

"Yes, sorry. I was just thinking. So the ring is bonded on and continues to be for as long as the participant is having regular sex?"

"Or unless they let me know they want to withdraw from the study," I remind him. "I remove the rings upon request, of course."

"Of course. I'm going to pass on your details to my friend, and I'm pretty sure he'll be in touch, but I don't know that he'll necessarily want to drop out. So don't worry too much about that. The whole ring-being-stuck thing didn't seem to bother him as much as it bothered his family."

That's not as reassuring as he seems to think it is. "I'll wait to hear from him."

"I'd also like to set up an appointment to discuss your research in more detail. Am I correct in thinking that if you had more funding, you'd be able to publish sooner?"

My vocal cords freeze, and for a second I can only manage a wordless squeak. Can he possibly mean what I think he means?

"Yes," I choke out. "Uhm. I'd use the funding to advertise more widely for participants, perhaps offer a small stipend for their participation. And hire a research assistant to help me with the data analysis. But more participants is the key factor. I have just under two thousand now, but the bigger the pool of data, the better. I'd love to at least double that. I think I can, if I had the funds to promote the study more."

"I agree. Are you able to come to the CSG offices so we can discuss it further?"

"Yes." *When? Now?* I manage to hold back those words, not wanting to seem overeager. Or desperate.

"Great. How about…" There's a pause, and I imagine him checking his calendar. "A week from next Tuesday at eleven?"

"Absolutely," I assure him. "I'll be there."

"Wonderful. I'm going to give you my email address, and I'd appreciate if you could send me an overview of your research. Whatever you use for participants is fine."

I scrabble for a pen and write down the email address he tells me, then give him my phone number so his friend —who I'm almost positive is Fabian Draco—can call me.

By the time he ends the call, I'm slightly dazed and

my hands are shaking. I'm not sure if that was a good professional experience or a terrible one.

But I have an appointment to discuss my research with the deputy head of our government. There's nothing bad about that.

I'm still sitting at my desk, staring at the phone, when Sura sticks her head around the door. "Oh good, you're done. So?" She comes in and leans against her desk.

"I'm not sure exactly what's going on," I say honestly, then recap the call for her.

"Wow. This is exciting! A meeting at CSG could be great for your research."

I nod slowly. "Yeah, but I don't know what to expect. How do I plan for this? What even is this?"

Practical as always, she rolls her eyes. "Start by sending him the info he wanted. Then just assume that the meeting will be a pitch. You know this study inside out, so that's not going to be a problem. Have some of your interim results ready in case he asks about them. This isn't scary, Rhys. You could take this meeting with your eyes closed."

I don't bother to tell her that makes no sense, just nod again and wake up my laptop. "Email first." I can do this.

IN ALL THE excitement of planning for my meeting at CSG, I forgot about David's "friend." Okay, I didn't actually forget. I just… immersed myself in the river called denial and pretended it was all going to be okay.

He wasn't going to call, and my research wouldn't be affected.

Ostriches have nothing on me.

My hopes were all for naught, though, because he called the next morning. I'd taken a break and gone out to get coffee, because even though KRD is a state-of-the-art facility with billions in funding, the coffee in the break rooms is garbage. Sura thinks it's deliberate to keep costs down, because if we don't drink it, they don't have to pay for it. That sounds like the kind of diabolical thing the finance department would come up with.

Anyway, I'm just strolling back into the office with my caramel latte, pondering all the ways the world would be improved if I started adding caramel to all my food, when Sura glances up at me from my desk and says into the phone, "He's just walked in. Could you hold for a moment? Thanks." She hits a button on the cordless handset and then holds it out to me, getting up from my chair. "Someone who says they're part of your study. I didn't get his name. He was kind of vague."

Annnnnd just like that, I'm forced to face reality. "Thanks," I tell her, taking the handset and putting down my coffee. Not even the caramel syrup can lift my mood right now.

I sit at my desk and bring up the participant files on my laptop, then take the call off hold and lift the handset to my ear. "This is Dr. Griffiths." Maybe if I sound professional and competent, he'll be encouraged to stay in the program.

"Hi… Dr. who? I mean, I know you're not Dr. Who. That would be so cool though. You're not, are you?"

Not… what? I try again. "I'm Dr. Rhys Griffiths."

"Ohhhh, Griffiths. That's of Welsh origin, right?

Medieval? Wales has such a fascinating history. Are you from there? Could I ask you some questions?"

What's even happening right now? I look over at Sura, who's watching me questioningly, and shrug. "I am Welsh, yes, but I haven't lived there for nearly seventy years. I'm sorry, what was your name?"

"Fabian Draco," he says dismissively. "So do you know much about Welsh history? I bet you know more than you think you do. If I put together a list of questions, would you go through it with me?"

"I… I suppose so. I don't know how helpful I'd be, though. There are certainly better sources you could speak with," I reply weakly, disappointed anew to learn that it really is him calling, not someone else the way a tiny part of me was still hoping. I try to rally my brain back to what's important. "Was there a reason you called?" It's ruder than I've ever been on the phone before, but I have the feeling that Fabian will wander off topic very easily… and then stay off topic.

"A reason? Uh, yes. Welsh—"

"Not about Welsh history," I break in hurriedly. "Before you knew I'm Welsh, you had a reason for calling. Maybe about the study I'm running? With the ring?"

"Are you the man who gave me my lovely ring? It was naughty of you not to tell me that humans think purity and chastity are the same thing, you know. I had to find out the hard way."

The… hard way? Is that an innuendo? "I… I didn't realize you didn't know. I'm sorry?" Did I really just apologize for something that's not my fault? Maybe it's a good thing he was vague and inattentive the first time we met. Who knows what I would have ended up agreeing to otherwise.

"Don't worry about it," he assures me. "It all worked out okay. But can I keep my ring?"

I take a deep breath. "Could we just confirm some things? I want to make sure I understand what we're talking about."

"We're talking about my ring," he says patiently. If only it was that simple.

"Yes. The ring I gave you when you signed up to participate in my study on the effect of regular sex on metaphysical health. That ring monitors your baseline health and your health during sex or sexual activity and sends the information to me. For my research."

"Ohhhhhhh," he says. "Is that what it's for? I thought it was just a pretty ring."

I close my eyes and resist the urge to bang my head against the desk. "I did explain all this when I gave you the ring," I remind him. "And I gave you a paper copy too."

"I remember you telling me stuff, don't worry," he assures me. "Is this why the ring won't come off?"

"That's right." I dredge up my patience. "To avoid contaminating the data—for example, if you lost it and someone else started wearing it, or if a friend wanted to try it on—the ring is bonded to your finger for as long as you're having regular sex. If you stop having sex for three months, the weaves become inert, and the ring can be removed. Or if you choose to cease participation in the study, I can remove the ring for you."

"Why would I want to stop participating? This sounds like interesting and important work. Have I been helpful? If I'd remembered what it was for, I could have tried to have more sex."

My jaw drops. Holy crap, I have incubi signed up who don't have sex as much as he does.

"No, that's… fine. You've been… very helpful. So, just to be clear, you're happy to continue with the study?"

"Oh yes. Now that I know why the ring won't come off, there's no problem. Do you need more participants? I know some people who might be interested."

"That would be amazing," I say honestly, overcome with relief that he doesn't want to pull out. "Just have anyone who's interested contact me. I'm happy to answer any questions they have if they're unsure."

"That's great. Okay, thanks!"

I open my mouth to reply, but I'm listening to the dial tone. What the fuck actually just happened?

I turn off the handset, put it down, pick up my coffee, and take a huge gulp. I need the caffeine and sugar to work some kind of miracle on my brain.

"Everything okay?" Sura asks. "That sounded kind of weird."

I turn my head to meet her gaze. "You have no idea."

CHAPTER THREE

Fabian

I CHECK the questions on my list one more time. There are more than I'd planned to have for this first meeting, but once I got started, I just couldn't limit myself. It's not like he has to answer them all today. I'll leave the list with him, and he can just email me later. My focus should be on the American literature paper I'm supposed to be writing or the memories I need to index for the living archive, anyway, not on Welsh history and culture.

"Are we going in or not?" Dustin asks impatiently. The only reason I could even drag him here is because the love of his life, Professor Sarris—no, I can call him Rob now—has classes all afternoon. I had to swear we'd be back in time for them to have dinner together. I still don't fully understand what they're doing. Dustin says they're getting to know each other, but there's no sex allowed because of Rob's ethics, and I have to chaperone them. Chaperonage is new to me—I didn't even know it existed until we moved to Earth—and I'm not sure if I'm very good at it. I mostly browse through

Rob's books and work while they do whatever they're doing in the other room. Based on the nineteenth-century literature I've been reading, I should be keeping a closer eye on them, but honestly, I think this no-sex thing they're doing is stupid, and if they don't have the willpower to keep from fucking, I'm not going to stop them.

I'd rather they didn't do it while I'm trying to concentrate, though. I might bring some noise-cancelling headphones next time, just in case they succumb to temptation.

"We're going in," I confirm. "You should definitely sign up for this study. You'll be helping people by having sex!" I think. I might have zoned out a little while Dr. Welshman explained it yesterday. His voice has such a nice lilt, and I was thinking of my questions about Wales and Welsh culture. David had already told me there was no danger to keeping the ring on and that he thinks the research is worthwhile. The only reason I even called was because Percy and Brandt said I should. I'm glad I did, since now I have a source for my Welsh research.

"I'm not having sex right now," Dustin snaps. He's been a little tense this week, probably because he's spending every possible free minute with Rob but not having sex. That would make me tense too.

"But you will," I soothe. "You and Rob will have alll-llll the sex. Inventive sex. Sleepy sex. Missionary sex. Hey, why's it called that? I've been meaning to ask for a long time and keep forgetting."

Dustin blinks at me. "I don't know. It has to be something to do with missionaries, right? And they're religious people. So maybe it's some kind of religious rite? Like that's the position they had to use when they had sex in the church on a holy day in front of the whole congregation?"

I think about it. "That sounds right. It would be a rite to draw their god's attention to the congregation and increase fertility in the community. Maybe it's seasonal—in the spring and the autumn, to bless the crops and harvest."

"That's sensible. You'd want a fertile harvest," Dustin agrees. "We should try to confirm this, though. There are probably a lot of little details."

"Let's go inside. Someone here probably knows. Scientists love to learn religious theories so they can explain why they're wrong." I lead the way into the building, which is all sleek and modern and science-y. There's a muted buzz to the reception area, the kind that tells me they're very busy but consider themselves too important and classy to speak loudly. Earth habits are fascinating.

I stroll up to the desk and smile at the receptionists. They're both on the phone, but the man—a shifter, if I'm guessing right—makes eye contact with me and smiles back. A moment later, he ends his call and turns all his attention to me.

"Can I help you?" There's a flirty vibe to the question. It doesn't surprise me—most people flirt with me, even those who don't want to take it further. I've been told there's something about me that just invites flirtation. Which is good, since I like sex and usually flirting comes first.

"Hi! We're here to see Dr. Welshman."

The shifter frowns and glances toward his colleague, but she's still on the phone. "Dr. Welshman? I don't think there's anybody by that name here. Are they visiting?"

I roll my eyes and smack myself in the forehead. "No, I'm sorry. His name is Dr. Griffiths. But he's a Welshman, see, and I'm interested in Welsh culture, so…" His eyes have glazed, so I force myself back to the point. "Could you point us in his direction? Dr. Griffiths's, I mean." I smile winningly.

The shifter blinks a few times, then makes a valiant attempt to rally. "Uh… is, uh, is he expecting you?"

"He should be."

"What was your name?" He glances at his computer screen and clicks his mouse.

"Fabian Draco. And this is Dustin Draco."

The shifter frowns again, looking at the screen. "You're not on the visitor list for today. Let me just…" He clicks a few more times. "And I don't see an appointment in his calendar. Are you sure he's expecting you?"

"Of course." He must be, right? I told him I had questions for him, and it's been a whole day since then.

"I'll just call and let him know you're here."

"Thank you."

He taps his headset, then presses some buttons on the funny-looking console in front of him. I've seen those before—it's called a switchboard, and the receptionist at CSG taught me how to use it when she was training Daíthí, the elf who's now the receptionist for the DEA. It's fascinating. The reason it's called a switchboard is because the original design, nearly a hundred and fifty years ago, used actual switches to connect phone calls. It's so amazing to think that Earth technology has gone from that to wireless telecommunications in such a short time.

"Dr. Griffiths? You have visitors. Fabian and Dustin Draco. Yes, of course. Thank you." He taps his headset again and gestures to a small seating area off to the side. "He's coming right out. Have a seat."

"Thanks!" I tug Dustin along. "Did you notice that we couldn't hear the other side of the conversation? That headset must have some special insulation or something. I wonder if we could get something like that."

"What for?" Dustin asks, dropping into a tub chair. "Also, the receptionist can hear you."

I look over my shoulder and see that the shifter is indeed watching us, so I twiddle my fingers in a little wave. He lifts his hand to wave back, then jerks it down and turns his attention back to his computer. "To see how they work, of course," I explain to Dustin. He's one of my dearest friends, but sometimes he's too focused on *now* instead of on all the things that came before and all the things we need to preserve for the future. "What led someone to develop them? How did they do it? Are they planning to make them widely available or keep them for a select few? Why? There are so many elements to learn about each simple thing."

He doesn't look convinced.

"Mr. Draco?" I turn at the sound of the familiar, lilting voice and see a man walking toward us. He's slightly above average height, with ashy-blond hair and green eyes. Green eyes are very unusual, and I mentally add some questions to my list. Is the color more prevalent amongst the Welsh? Does it represent his Welsh heritage, or does it descend from an ancestor of a different cultural background who married into Wales?

How many people in his family have the same eye color? Is it exactly the same, that clear, intense green that almost looks fake, or are their eyes a slightly different shade?

"Hi! You must be Dr. Welshman… I mean, Dr. Griffiths. Please call me Fabian." I hold out my hand to shake in the Earth custom. I really like this habit—it allows my magic to get the measure of every person I meet. Not that I'd ever tell anyone I'm doing that. Technically, it's rude to scan people with magic unless they give permission, even a surface-level scan.

"It's nice to see you again, Fabian," he says warily. "Did I know you were coming in today?"

I don't answer for a second, too busy being surprised by the strength of his shielding. It's sorcery, of course, rather than the dragon magic I use, but it still locks him down tight. I'd have to *try* to break through it, and I'm not sure I would succeed… plus, I'd probably damage him in the attempt.

"Fabian?" Dustin says, and I realize they're both staring at me.

"Yes. No. Um… maybe? I did tell you I had questions." He seems surprised, so I hurry on, "This is Dustin, and he's interested in signing up to your study. But he won't be having sex for another week and a half. Is that okay?"

"Ten and a half more days," Dustin corrects gloomily.

The doctor looks kerflummoxed, which is an amazing word I learned from the administrator in the dean's office at school. It means confused, but on a slightly more in-depth level. "That's fine. I don't expect you to be, uh, engaging in sexual activity all the time.

Why don't we go somewhere more private where I can explain the study to you?"

"And look at my questions," I add. He better not forget about that part.

"Sure," he agrees, but he looks unsure. Shaking his head slightly, he adds, "Just give me a moment," then goes over to the reception desk and asks the shifter if a meeting room is available. A minute later, he's ushering us down a hall and into a small room with a round table, a wall-mounted television, and a console table with a pod-style coffee machine on it.

"This is perfect!" I announce, then point to the TV. "Will that link up with my phone?"

"Yes," he says. I ignore the reluctance in his tone. Many people sound that way before an interview with me, but I've learned to persevere. My job is to document and preserve knowledge, and I'll get it done even if nobody wants to help.

"Fabian, why don't you get that set up and go over your questions one more time while Dr. Griffiths explains his study to me?" Dustin suggests, and the doctor smiles in relief.

"Please, call me Rhys," he says.

"That would definitely be better than Fabian calling you Dr. Welshman all the time."

"He's a Welshman *and* a doctor. It fits," I insist, even though I agree with him. It was starting to get awkward. "Rhys is a very Welsh name too. How do you spell it?"

He spells it out for me, and then Dustin interrupts again. I decide to go ahead and link my phone to the TV so Rhys can see all my questions. They're still talking when I'm done, so I occupy myself searching through the online archive the community has been slowly putting together. It's painstaking work to photograph, scan, or transcribe nine thousand years' and more worth of history, but they're getting it done. When Noah, who works with David at CSG, introduced me to some of the archivists and told them what my job is, they very kindly offered me access to their history. And now that Brandt has said I can run a class on dragon culture, I know they'll be excited to help me plan the course material.

I skim through the index of new uploads, bookmarking a few to look at later—I *really*_like Mesopotamian history—and then click into one of the "ancient" folklore files I've been reading. The thing I find most interesting about these is that a lot of the stories are based on handed-down tales from when we dragons and the elves were visiting Earth through portals—back before the travel ban. I wasn't alive then, but I heard lots of stories about Earth while I was growing up. We had no idea that their knowledge of us was lost to time, thanks to the drama of the species wars. Until we came back five years ago, they had no idea that all this folklore was based—very loosely based—in fact.

Like the one I'm reading now, which portrays elves as sneaky little mischief-makers. The truth is, while some elves are fun, most of them have an overinflated sense of responsibility. We dragons are much more laid-back.

"Fabian?"

I drag myself back to the present. Dustin and Dr. Rhys are looking at me.

"All done with your sex experiment?" I ask brightly, and for some reason, the doctor winces.

"It's not a sex experiment," he begins, but I wave him off.

"Oh, I know. It's very important. I've read a lot of research that proves the link between orgasm and endorphin release. It makes sense that the community would have magic endorphins as well as regular ones."

"Do we have endorphins?" Dustin wonders. "We're not Earth species."

"We do. They work a bit differently from the ones Earth species have, though. I don't really understand it. Sophie tried to explain it to me once, but I got bored."

He pats my hand. "Of course you did. Sophie's explanations always get too technical and science-y. I'm going to get a coffee while you ask Rhys all your questions. Do you want something?"

"There's coffee right there." I point to the machine, and Dustin gives me a pitying look.

"I want something milky and frothy with flavored syrup that I don't have to make myself."

Ooh, now that he mentions it, that does sound good. "Hazelnut cappuccino, please." I looooove cappuccinos. They don't have much of that icky coffee flavor, but there's lots of frothy milk. Coffee is really not that good plain, but when you add enough milk and syrup, it's delightful.

He grins at me cheekily and saunters out, closing the door firmly behind him.

I smile at Dr. Rhys, who looks wary for some reason, and pat the chair beside me. "Come, sit. This is going to be fun!"

He obediently switches chairs, then says, "I'm really not sure if I'll be of any use to you. There are many other people who know a lot more about Welsh culture and history than I do."

"That's okay." I pat his arm reassuringly. "I'm sure you'll do the best you can."

He swallows, so I pat him again. His forearm is really nicely shaped under his shirt. Lots of definition. More than a scientist usually has. "Do you do… exercising stuff?" I watch TV. I know that people have to move weights around and other things to get muscles. The dragon way is much easier and involves no sweat. The only good reason to sweat that I can think of is sex.

He side-eyes me. "Are you asking if I work out?"

I snap my fingers. "That's how you say it! Yes. Do you? Because your forearm feels lovely. Roll up your sleeve so I can see."

His jaw drops, drawing my attention to his face. He's really quite attractive. Good bone structure. Not that I'm picky about how people look. It's more about their manner than anything else. I want someone who'll be fun in bed.

Speaking of bed…

"Do you know why the missionary position is called that?"

There's an audible click as his jaw snaps shut, and a wave of color flushes his face. "Uh, is this a joke? Because while I'm sure it's funny—"

"No, I'm not joking," I declare earnestly. "Dustin and I were talking about it before. Why is it called the missionary position? Is it because missionaries used to do it that way in rites when they were inducting new people into their church?"

He stares at me, screws his eyes closed, then opens them and says, "No. I'm not entirely sure why it's called the missionary position, but I can assure you that any human religion that has missionaries is not conducting sex rites."

I sigh. "That's disappointing. I've been thinking about studying human religions—when I'm finished with my English degree—and sex rites would have been fascinating."

"Fascinating. Yes. That's… a word for it."

"Do you know anyone who might know the origin of the missionary position? I guess I could just google it, but I'd much rather get the information from an expert. Maybe I could contact some religious organizations."

"You could try, but I think most of them don't take too kindly to inquiries about sex. They might think you're playing a joke on them. I-I can ask a friend of mine who's an anthropologist if he knows."

"Oooh!" I grin. "An anthropologist. I'd like to meet him, please. He could help me a lot with my research on humans."

Dr. Rhys looks a bit dazed, but he nods. "I'll talk to him and let you know."

"Great! Now, you never answered my question. Do you work out? Can I see your muscles?"

He swallows. "That's probably not appropriate."

I blink, confused. "Why not? We're going to have sex. Why can't I see your arms?"

He shoves his chair back and scrambles to his feet so fast, I can almost still feel his arm under my hand.

"We—what—we're—why…" He stops and sucks in a deep breath. "We're not going to have sex. Why would you think that? That would be so inappropriate and… and *bad*."

"Excuse you, sex with me is *never* bad!" How dare he!

"And why wouldn't we have sex? Are you in a relationship?"

"Would you care if I said yes?"

This is just too insulting. "Of course I'd care! Unless it's a consensual poly relationship, in which case I have no qualms about fucking you. But otherwise, I don't get involved with people who are attached. Not anymore. One time, the girlfriend I had no idea existed tracked me down with a knife and told me I had to go with her, and when I tried to put down the scroll I was reading first, she *ripped it out of my hands*. It was damaged beyond repair." I shake my head sadly at the memory. "After that, I knew it wasn't worth fucking people who aren't single."

Dr. Rhys is staring at me like I'm a particularly fascinating piece of heretofore lost history. "Did she harm you?"

"Who?"

"The girlfriend with the knife!"

He completely missed the point of that story. "Oh. Yes. She stabbed me twice in the side before someone heard her shouting and came to help."

He nods slowly and drops into his chair, two feet away from the table. "You're obviously okay now."

I wave a hand. "Healing people is easy. But scrolls and books..." I tsk and shake my head. "That poor scroll."

"Yes, the... scroll. I can see why that would have been traumatic for you."

"It really was. But you're not dating anyone or married, and I'm sure you'd never damage a historic document—would you?"

He shakes his head.

"Excellent. So we can have sex, then."

He shakes his head again, and I sigh. "Why not? Are you not into men?" Surely I haven't missed something like that. I'm normally excellent at guessing when men are open to a same-sex experience, even if they've never had one before and never planned to. For a few centuries back home, I was known locally as First-Time Fabian because of all the guys who had their first gay sex experience with me.

"That's not relevant," he says calmly. He seems to have gotten his composure back. "You're a participant in my research study. It would be unethical for me to have sex with you."

I groan. I've been hearing way too much lately about sex being unethical. That's why Dustin and Rob aren't fucking like bunnies right now: because Rob doesn't want to be unethical. It's so dumb—Dustin's not the usual twenty-year-old student who's subject to Rob's grading in order to finish college and get a career. Dustin's only at college because it sounded like fun! And now this.

"How is it unethical for us to have sex? What impact would it have on your research or my life?"

He opens his mouth and then closes it again.

"Exactly. This isn't a drug trial or a medical treatment, where a personal connection between us could impact the outcome of my health or the results. Hypothetically, I could have met you on the street and picked you up without us recognizing each other from our one short meeting four years ago. Why is it so different if you know who I am?"

"Well… it just is. You're a participant," he says weakly, pinching the bridge of his nose.

I roll my eyes. "Yeah, yeah. I think that's a stupid reason. If you don't want to fuck me, fine. I can accept that. But if you're down for it and the only thing stopping you is the study, that's silly. I could drop out, if that makes it easier. But I want to keep my ring," I add. No way am I letting him take it away from me.

"If you want to drop out," he says slowly, "you can do so at any time. But I'd—" He stops and clenches his jaw.

"You'd what?" I watch the muscles ticking, fascinated. He has a lovely jawline. I usually like men with a bit of scruff, but his jaw is really too nice to cover up. I wonder how he'd react if I kissed him right *there*, at the hinge.

"Ethically," he begins, and I sigh. "*Ethically*, I can't attempt to convince you to stay in the study if you want to drop out. If you say you want to end your participation, the only ethical route open to me is to say 'okay' and make that happen."

It takes me a moment to understand why he's so uncomfortable. Aww, look at him, compromising his ethics so he can hint that he wants me to stay in the program.

"But if I keep participating, your other ethics say we can't have sex." I widen my eyes and bat my eyelashes like Dustin does all the time. I don't have that same adorable vibe he does, but it's worth a try.

Dr. Rhys frowns. "Are you okay?"

Hmm. I guess I can't pull that off. I'll just have to rely on my natural sexual magnetism. "I'm fine. Just had an eyelash or dust or something. All better now. So... where do we stand on having sex?"

"It's not happening," he says firmly. "But if you want to drop out of the study, I can arrange that."

"Pfft. If you won't have sex with me, there's no point dropping out. Will you at least take off your shirt… no?" The look he's giving me would cause a lesser being to quail. "What about rolling up your sleeves so I can see your forearms?"

Shaking his head, he says, "If you want to ask me questions while I'm fully dressed, let's get on with it. Otherwise, I've got to get back to work. You can wait here for Dustin to come back."

What a party pooper. "Fiiiiiiine. Let's talk about Wales."

He rolls his chair back over to the table and sits beside me, but not close enough for things to be fun. I'm only pouting a little bit when I activate the TV and begin walking him through my questions. Just as I suspected, he knows more than he thinks he does, and even when he's unsure, he gives me enough information to determine which paths I should go down.

Dustin comes back with coffee for all of us, and it's sooooo good, with hardly any coffee at all. I smile at him gratefully.

Then he ruins it by demanding to know when we can leave. "I need to be back for dinner with Rob," he whines like a whiny baby who whines a lot.

Dr. Rhys begins to stand. "If you need to go, I'd be happy to email you the rest—"

"We don't need to go," I snap, glaring at Dustin. "There's plenty of time, and I'm almost done. Just because you're not getting any doesn't mean I shouldn't."

They both pause.

"I don't want to watch you have sex," Dustin says.

"We're not having sex!" Dr. Rhys insists. "It would be unethical!"

Dustin gives me a sympathetic look. "Oh, you too? That sucks. See if you can negotiate him down to two weeks, like I did with Rob."

"There's no need for that. I would never pressure Dr. Rhys into having sex with me when he so clearly doesn't want to. There's plenty of time for him to change his mind organically. I'm playing the long game." I hesitate. "What does that mean, exactly?"

Dr. Rhys, who'd relaxed a little when I began speaking but then tensed up again at the end, says, "It means being patient and waiting for something that might not happen for a long time. But let me reiterate, I'm not going to have sex with you."

"Not even when the study's over?"

He opens his mouth to retort—probably something about his ethics—then closes it again.

"It's good that you're not going to pressure him," Dustin says gravely. "Willing consent is so important."

"I know, right? I can be patient. It's not like I'm going to get old or die unless I want to. And I'm sure Dr. Rhys has a few hundred years left."

"Closer to a thousand," he declares indignantly.

I clap my hands. "Great! So we have plenty of time. You focus on your study for now, and when the time is right, it'll happen."

He starts to sputter, and Dustin leans over to murmur, "I think you broke him."

"Nah, he's just processing. Look how cute he is like this. I love when brainy people discover they can't brain their way through everything."

Dustin purses his lips. "I don't think that's how you say it."

"But you knew what I meant, so it's fine. That's how language evolves." I nod solemnly. "I know because I did some research into the evolution of language about a thousand years ago."

"A *thousand*… How old even are you?" Dr. Rhys demands.

"Isn't that considered a rude question here on Earth, Dr. Rhys?"

"You can just call me Rhys, you know. Or Dr. Griffiths. Dr. Rhys makes me sound like a cut-rate talk show host."

I'm not sure exactly what he means by that, but he sounds all grumpy and impatient, and it makes me hot. Men who easily get grumpy—not mad, just grumpy— are always so much fun in bed.

"But I like calling you Dr. Rhys. You earned your doctorate and alllllll the *authority* that goes with it," I smile wickedly, "but I don't want to call you Dr. Griffiths, because that's too formal. You and I aren't going to be formal like that… Dr. Rhys."

He takes a deep breath and then heaves it out in a big sigh. "Sure. Just… don't call me that in front of my colleagues?"

I shrug. "Okay. And to answer your question, I'm nearly four and a half thousand years old."

He stares. "Nearly?"

"My conversion from our cycle to your year might be a little bit off. It's near enough, though."

His Adam's apple bobs as he swallows. "You seem much younger. Much, much younger."

"We dragons are very laid-back and young at heart.

That's why we fit in so well everywhere we go. We don't take ourselves too seriously."

Dustin nods in agreement. "You should think about that," he adds. "Standards of ethics change over time. What was ethical five hundred years ago is different from today, and it will be different again in five hundred more. The only thing that remains static is whether your actions will cause harm. If they don't, then who cares about the rules?"

Dr. Rhys's eyes bulge, and even I think Dustin might be pushing things. Rules are a keystone of civilized societies. Sure, sometimes they don't make sense, and yes, few of them are immutable. Time changes nearly everything. But most people need rules to feel secure. That's why so many humans turn to religion, even though it's so patently false. It's fascinating. One day, I'll study human religions and the dependence people have on them.

"Let's worry about that another day," I say soothingly. "I think we've taken up enough of Dr. Rhys's time. He's very busy studying sex. I'm going to email you the rest of these questions, Dr. Rhys, and you get back to me when you can. But you should come out to the estate the weekend after next. We're having a small party, and I think there will be a lot of people there who'd be interested in signing up to your study." And he'll be able to see me in a more casual environment. Of course he's not going to relax his stupid ethics while we're in his place of work. That would be like taking me to a frat party and asking me to swear off sex. Please. All those horny frat boys looking to try something new? It's a smorgasbord.

"I'm not sure…," Dr. Rhys says, but he looks torn. I

know he really wants more participants for his study, but he's probably worried he won't be able to resist me.

"You don't need to decide now. I'm sure you need to check your schedule anyway. I'll email the details." I disconnect my phone from the TV, hop up from my chair, tuck it back in, then grab my half-full coffee with one hand and pat Dr. Rhys's arm—his bicep this time— with the other. He really does have lovely arms. I only wish I could have seen them. "You take care now, and we'll see you soon!"

We leave him standing in the meeting room with a kerflummoxed expression and make our way back to reception, waving at the receptionists on our way out. Dustin waits until we're back to the car before he says, "Sometimes I think you're an evil genius. Then you do something like tie your shoelaces before you put the shoes on your feet, and I'm not sure what you are."

"That only happened one time," I protest, even though it's more like six times. He only knows about one, though, and that's what's important. I can't be expected to pay attention to petty details like whether I'm wearing my shoes when I'm responsible for preserving the history and knowledge of all dragonkind. At least I remembered to tie the shoelaces.

That doesn't matter anyway. My focus now needs to be on all the ways I can teach the Earth species about dragons… and researching how the missionary position got its name. Oh, and having lots of sex to help Dr. Rhys with his study so he can finish it sooner and we can fuck.

A dragon's gotta have goals.

CHAPTER FOUR

Rhys

AFTER THE DRAGONS LEAVE, I stay in the meeting room for a few minutes more, staring at the door and trying to process. It's not easy. I'm not even entirely sure what just happened. Did I commit to having sex with Fabian at some time in the future? I don't think I did, but he seems so certain it's going to happen….

Not that it would be a hardship. I've never in my life met anyone so casually certain of their own appeal. And he's so sex positive. The community isn't like humans, who are way more prudish about sex, but we're not as freely sexual as Fabian seems to be.

Shaking my head, I flip off the lights in the meeting room and head back to the lab. I need sensible data to help me get my head on straight again. These dragons are tricky.

Sura's waiting for me, and I wince. I wish I'd thought to have Chris call and tell her what was happening. All she knows is that the dragon from my study who caused the call from CSG turned up unannounced.

"Well? What happened? You were gone ages, but

you didn't come back to get any paperwork, so he can't have dropped out."

"He didn't," I confirm. "He actually brought a friend who wants to sign up. I have to email him the consent form." I pat my pocket where my phone is. Dustin gave me his contact information, and I want to send the form out as soon as possible. I don't think he'll change his mind, though. Unlike Fabian, he had some very insightful questions while I was explaining the study, and he seemed very interested in the impact this kind of research could have.

"That's great!" Sura grins widely, but it fades as she eyes me. "Why aren't you happier?"

I wasn't planning to tell anyone about Fabian's proposition. I really wasn't. But when faced with the intent gaze of my closest friend, I can't hold it in. At least I still have the presence of mind to make sure we're the only ones in the lab before I start my word vomit.

Her jaw drops before I reach the halfway point, and when I finally conclude with Dustin inviting me to the dragon estate a few hours from here in the country, she's slumped in a chair.

"Wow," she whispers.

"Right? This is so awkward."

"It really is." There's a short silence while we both ponder the difficulty of my current situation. "You're going to sleep with him, though, right?"

"What? No!" I sputter. "Sura!"

She shrugs, straightening in the chair and gliding back and forth on the casters. "Why not? He's right about that, at least. The standard of ethics you're applying to this study is higher than needed. It's purely observational. You're not administering any drugs or conducting any procedures; you haven't even had any contact with any of your participants since they signed up. I can't imagine anyone who would consider this to be *actually* unethical."

She's right, and I hate that. Because *yes*, Fabian is attractive, and if we'd met in a bar, I would have had no hesitation in following him back to his place or my car or the men's room. But in a situation like that, we probably wouldn't have talked much. It would have been BJs or handies or a rushed fuck, and then we would have gone our separate ways.

That's impossible now. Well, for me it is, anyway. I'm a stage-ten clinger once I get to know someone, and I already know more about Fabian than I did about my last boyfriend. I know he's hard core into history and learning about different cultures. I know he loves rings and, at a guess, probably collects them. I know he's intelligent, attractive, highly sexual, and sweet-natured. He's blunt almost to a fault, but not mean. He respects my decision even though he doesn't understand it, and he's not going to let it stop us from being friends if I'm okay with that.

What it comes down to is that I like him, and if we fuck on top of that, I'll probably start getting feelings. It's tough being a romantic. Shit like this happens to me *all* the time. And while Fabian seems to be a nice guy, I'm not sure he's looking for feelings. So I'll end up with a bruised heart again.

On the flip side, he might turn out to be such an asshole that it never gets to that. I've been through that a few times too. Lots of fun.

When I look up, Sura is watching me sympathetically. "It might turn out okay this time," she suggests.

She's been there with me through a lot of the shitstorm that is my dating life. "And even if it just turns out to be a good time for a little while, you need that. It's been ages since you got any."

"Not that long," I mutter defensively.

She snorts. "Yes, that long. You're doing a study on the effects of sex on metaphysical health, and you don't qualify to participate, it's been that long."

Yeah. She's right. In fact, technically I've never been eligible to participate. At first I was so focused on getting things set up that I put all thoughts of sex on the back burner. Then I was distracted by the data coming in… and then something else came up… and then it just seemed like too much effort. So, yeah, if I put one of those rings on, it would deactivate without ever transmitting more than baseline data.

I sigh. How did my life come to this? I'm a young sorcerer—still under two hundred. I should be living it up.

"You don't have to decide now," Sura says softly. "Get through the meeting at CSG, then go to the dragon party, sign some people up, and check this Fabian guy out in his natural habitat." She pauses, pursing her lips. "Isn't 'Fabian' a song title?"

I shrug, still thinking about the wasteland that is my sex life. "Is it? You know I don't follow music that much."

"I'm sure it is. It's one of those human comedy songs. It was a… well, not really a Christmas song. I think it was a parody? Because the humans have a Christmas song about a reindeer. And this was also a song about a reindeer. Called Fabian. Who was inbred.

And… if I remember right, his father was also his sister."

That gets my attention, and I look up. "What?"

She spreads her hands. "It's been a while since I've heard it, but I think that's how it goes. And then the Fabian reindeer eats his father/sister."

I blink slowly. "Why are you telling me this?"

"If you're going to fuck a guy called Fabian, you have to be prepared for all eventualities."

"I don't know why I bother talking to you."

To say I'm shocked when I walk into my meeting at CSG and find it's not just with David Carew, but also Imani Abara, the CSG health liaison, and a bunch of other people, is an understatement. Here at the CSG office, away from human eyes, nobody's bothered with glamor, and the three strangers are very obviously *other*. I've never been in an informal or truly private setting with an elf or dragon, so this is the first time I've seen their true features. The pointed ears, the sharp bone structure—high cheekbones, pointy chin, heavy brow bone. Their eye sockets are shaped differently from ours too. It's alien yet very appealing, and I'm suddenly glad Fabian kept his glamor up when we met the other day. It would have been a lot harder to say no to showing him my muscles if I'd seen his true face.

My nerves are back, and they ramp all the way up when David introduces the strangers as people from the DEA—the Dragon-Elf Alliance—an elf called Caoimhe and a dragon called Sophie, both of whom are their species' counterparts for Imani, and the wing leader of all freaking dragons, Brandt. My hand is trembling when I shake his. I can understand why the others are here, but not him. Isn't he too busy and important to be taking an interest in this so early in the process?

David must notice my confusion, because as he gestures me toward an empty chair, he says, "Brandt's here because he likes to stick his nose into other people's lives."

For a second, my heart stops beating, but then Brandt chuckles. "That's true," he agrees. "I had to meet the man who gave Fabian a purity ring."

I try not to wince. "You know Fabian?"

Brandt, who looks like a hot Daddy who's aging really well, nods. "Of course. I know all my dragons. But Fabian's our species historian and record keeper, so he lives at the estate."

I smile weakly. "I guess that explains why he was so curious about Welsh history."

Sophie laughs. "He's curious about everything. When he got home from his meeting with you, he disappeared into his rooms to research ancient human sex rites that were used to attract prosperity and health. I think you've given him a new hobby."

"I'm pretty sure sex has always been his hobby," Brandt says dryly. "At least now he's using it to help society."

That has to be one of the weirdest sentences I've ever heard.

David settles everyone down with a quiet word and explains to me that they've all seen the materials I sent and now have questions. What follows is just as intense as when I had to convince the board at KRD to grant me the funding for the study… and possibly also my doctoral defense. I'm so glad I spent time putting the data into easy-to-read charts and graphs for this meeting, because they want numbers, they want them broken down every which way, and they question everything.

It's kind of exhilarating.

Finally, there's a lull, and they glance at each other around the table, nodding subtly. I'm pretty sure that's a good sign, not code for "let's toss this whackjob out on his ass."

"Thank you, Dr. Griffiths," Imani says. "We appreciate your time today. Before we proceed, we'd like for you to sign a nondisclosure agreement."

They… what?

"A nondisclosure agreement?" I hope I don't sound as befuddled as I feel. "Uh… of course." Whatever they're about to tell me must be big. Or scary. Or big and scary. The scientist in me is thrilled.

The rest of me feels vaguely sick.

Imani slides a document over to me, and I take a few minutes to scan over it. It's pretty standard, and at a guess I'd say this is just a generic agreement they use for things that have to be kept confidential but won't end the world. I sign it and slide it back.

"Thank you," she says again. "Metaphysical health is something that hasn't gotten as much attention as it should over the past few centuries. There's been much more focus on physical and mental well-being, and we have data that shows the strength of our abilities has been waning slowly over time. We're working to identify the cause, but in the meantime we're interested in anything that might slow or reverse this issue before it's too late."

I try not to react externally, but it's a jolt to my

system. *Too late?* Does she mean before we lose our abilities entirely? How can this be? Our abilities are an intrinsic part of us. What would I do if I couldn't weave sorcery? It's not only an element of my job, it's also key to my identity.

"Oh," I manage. "I don't suppose I could have access to that?" The scientist in me needs to see proof.

She raises an eyebrow at David, who answers, "Some of it, at least. Perhaps down the track we can release the rest. It's tied in with other research that's highly classified."

"Of course." I swallow, not wanting to think about what kind of research would measure the strength of abilities and need to be classified. "So you think my study could potentially reverse this trend?" This is really fascinating. I hadn't realized my work would have such an important application. I was thinking along the lines of giving general health a nudge, the way a regular walk is good for physical fitness but can't cure illnesses. This could be so much more than that.

"We're not willing to overlook any research that might prove helpful right now," Imani says firmly. "We'd collectively," she gestures to the representatives from the other species, "like to fund your research and push it as far as it can go." She names a figure that makes my hands reflexively clench. With that money, I can expand the study by ten times. "We'll also publicly sponsor it to widen awareness and attract more participants."

I clear my throat and try not to let loose a victory shriek. "That's great news," I say calmly. "I assume that in return, you'd like full access to the results?" That's fine, of course. It will mean contacting existing participants and asking them to sign a release form, but even if they decline, the new participants this attracts will more than make up for the loss. Way more. Exponentially.

"Yes. They will, of course, be subject to our privacy laws and only used in accordance with such."

I want to say "Of course" and smile, but it seems my voice has failed me, so I just nod. She smiles kindly.

"I appreciate this is a lot to take in, especially since you weren't even expecting us to be here for this meeting. Why don't we leave it here for now? We can set up another meeting to discuss the details and how you plan to proceed."

Yes. Perfect. "That's a great idea. To be honest, I never expected to be able to scale up at this level, so there are some figures I'd like to check. But I do have one question." I turn to Caoimhe and Sophie. "Has this abatement of ability affected your species also? Or is it just community species?"

"The elves have been affected," Caoimhe says immediately. "We were somewhat preoccupied with more immediate issues"—she's referring to the impending collapse of their dimension, of course. I can see how that would have distracted them—"but once we were settled here and Imani brought the matter to our attention, we checked into some things and found there has been an impact."

"It seems to be slower than what we're seeing," Imani adds, "but we can't be sure why that is without understanding what's caused this. Which..." She shrugs. "We have no idea. We're hoping your research will provide some insights."

Wow. No pressure or anything. "Once I have a bigger sample size, we may have some unexpected discoveries," I say vaguely, then turn my attention to Sophie.

She shakes her head. "I have noticed no such change in dragons. There are far fewer of us, of course, and our origins are very different to all other species. Our abilities are also different. But we are determined to discover the source of this issue and see it resolved." She grins at Brandt. "And not just because our wing leader is a whiny baby when his paired soul is out of sorts."

It takes me a moment to work out that she's referring to Brandt's partner, Percy, who used to be the lucifer. He's a felid shifter, so of course this would affect him.

"I have three dragons in the study at the moment, as you saw. It would be helpful to understand more clearly the differences between you and other species. Especially the elves, since physically you're so alike."

Caoimhe snorts. "Not even that, I'm afraid."

I don't get it. Thankfully, Sophie explains before I have to ask.

"Dragons were originally ethereal beings of pure energy. The discovery of a physical body—our dragon form—was accidental, but we found we enjoyed it too much to give it up. It wasn't until we encountered the elves that we first shifted also into a biped form in order to communicate with them. We basically just copied their shape, but our genetic makeup is entirely different."

I have no idea what to say. My brain is bursting with questions.

Brandt laughs. "I know that expression. It's scientist face. You and Sophie will have plenty of time to talk about this."

"Definitely," Sophie says. "And you should talk to Fabian too. I've got the medical side covered, but he's got access to the living archive and can tell you exactly how it all went down."

I make a mental note to ask later about the living archive, because that sounds both super cool and super scary. "I'll put together a list of questions," I assure her. It almost comes out sounding like a threat, I'm that eager, and I get a round of chuckles.

"In the meantime, you should come out to the estate this weekend," she invites. "We're having a small gathering, and there will be lots of dragons and some elves and others there. It's a good opportunity to interest people in your research and get some more information."

"Good plan," Brandt approves. "Come for the whole weekend. You and Fabian and Sophie can talk about… things." He waves a hand to encompass all the "things" we're supposed to discuss. "You don't mind working on the weekend, do you? I'm sure you can take a day or two off next week in lieu."

I try not to think about when I last took a full weekend off. Was it in the spring? Or maybe that time last winter when the power went out at the lab and I couldn't work anyway. "I don't mind," I say absently, and somehow Brandt takes that as agreement and starts giving me directions to the dragon compound, which is called—get this—Here Be Dragons.

Someone had to be high when they picked that name. Either that or dragons are weird.

Before I know it, the meeting is breaking up. I'm given an assortment of business cards and hand out a bunch of my own—thank fuck I remembered to bring them—and then Brandt is reminding me to arrive in time for dinner on Friday night and they're all filing out of the meeting room.

Until it's just me and David left.

I look at him, a little surprised by how good-looking he is. I noticed before, of course, but my nerves and then finding all the other people here distracted me. But now he's smiling sympathetically at me, his dark-blue eyes alight, and I find myself smiling back.

"Did I just agree to spend the weekend with the dragons?" I ask, because I think I did but can't be entirely sure.

He nods. "Yeah. Don't worry, though. Percy will rescue you if you need it. And I'll be there for some of it." He hesitates. "Try not to get on Steffen's bad side, though."

Worry surfaces. "Is there anything in particular I should avoid?"

He shrugs. "Who knows? Just… go with it. And try not to be alone with him. The others are pretty good about keeping him in check, but he can be a bit hard to take on his own."

"Is he dangerous?" Do I remember any of the self-defense course I took a few decades back?

"Only to logic and reason. Come on, I'll introduce you to Noah. He's got the data you'll need."

By the time I get back to KRD, I'm mostly over my shock and getting super excited about all the opportunities ahead of me. I stop at reception and ask Chris to get me an urgent appointment with the director. "Make sure you tell him it's good news," I add. The last thing I need is to piss him off.

Chris looks bored and annoyed as usual as he clicks into the scheduling app to arrange it, and I head down the hallway toward my lab.

Only to feel let down when Sura isn't there. The two other researchers we share with are, and I like them both, but Sura will kill me if I tell them my news before her. Fortunately, I find her in the office, swearing like a sailor at something on her computer.

"Progress or expense reports?" I ask. Those are usually what piss her off.

"Neither," she bites out, still giving her screen a death glare. "That asshat in HR ate my yogurt, and now he has the nerve to deny it."

Ahhh, break room dramas. The joy of working in a shared space.

"I'll buy you a new yogurt if you'll pay attention to me."

She mutters a few more choice words about HR guy's personal hygiene, then reluctantly drags her eyes over to me. "What's up? Oh, you're back from your meeting!"

Yep, it took her that long to notice. What's that human expression? Hell hath no fury like a pissed-off Sura. "I am."

"How'd it go? Was he interested? Do you think you'll get a grant out of it? You could do so much with even just fifty grand."

"I'm definitely getting a grant." I smile widely, letting my glee take over, and then tell her everything. Well, almost everything. The part about us getting metaphysically weaker is top secret, so I skim over it. She interrupts half a dozen times, but only shrieks once.

"This is *amazing*," she says when I'm done.

"It's a fantastic opportunity," I admit.

"So is this weekend thing. It's the perfect chance for you and Fabian to hook up. I'm sure he knows all the private nooks and crannies in the house… and if not, there's always his bedroom."

Yeah, just gonna ignore that. Fortunately, the phone rings, and I lean over to grab it.

"It took some work," Chris declares without even saying hello, "but you have thirty minutes with the director right now. Don't keep him waiting." He hangs up before I can reply.

"Fuck. Gotta go see the director," I say over my shoulder as I head for the door. Sura just waves me off. Those of us who have low-budget, not-that-sexy research understand the imperative to stay on the director's good side.

I race through the halls while trying to look like I'm not racing, which results in a very uptight-looking waddling jog. If Fabian could see me now, he'd completely lose interest in having sex with me. Maybe I should try this over the weekend.

The director's assistant, a cool blonde vampire with enough brains and ambition to sink the *Titanic*, raises a brow when I enter her domain trying not to pant. I've never seen her lose her cool, not even when the firebug wandered into her office. She just calmly called for a general evac and then grabbed the fire extinguisher.

"He's waiting," she says, her tone implying that I'm deliberately dragging my feet to waste the director's valuable time. Even though she can clearly see I'm a disheveled mess after running through the whole facility.

"Thank you." I manage not to gasp the words, then knock lightly on the double doors and wait for the director's imperious "Yes."

Inside, the office is not as posh as everyone expects. There's no expensive art, no plush furnishings or ornate desk. The director may be tight with the purse strings—and he really is—but he doesn't spend money on himself either. I close the door behind me and take a seat opposite him. He's focused on his screen, tapping away at the keyboard, but I know from past experience that he's fully aware of me and that he wouldn't appreciate me hovering and waiting for an invitation to sit.

Finally he turns away from the computer and focuses on me. He's a demon, and a scientist, although truthfully, his research was only ever mediocre. But he understands our work processes, and he's an excellent administrator and businessman, making him the perfect director. Even if he does scare the living daylight out of me with his demon broodiness.

"What can I do for you, Dr. Griffiths? A matter of urgency that's not bad news, I believe."

"It's excellent news, sir. CSG is going to fund my research." I explain about the meeting and what the next steps will be.

His face portrays mild interest and curiosity. "That is good news. Though I have to say I'm surprised not to have been notified ahead of time that you had something like this in the works."

"I didn't, sir. I was expecting a preliminary discussion and possibly an invitation to apply for a grant. If I'd known what was coming, I would have asked you to attend with me." That's the truth, although I doubt the outcome would have been any different. It's not like I needed to negotiate anything.

He nods, accepting that, then questions me on a few of the details. When he eventually sits back, he's smiling. Well… smiling for him. On anyone else, you probably wouldn't think it was. "I'd like to see your plan once you have it laid out. Are you confident you can manage this weekend, or would you like me to wrangle an invitation also?"

Oh fuck no. The last thing I need my boss to see is Fabian's unsubtle come-ons.

"I'd welcome your company, sir, but I don't think I need it. Don't feel you have to give up your weekend for me."

To my astonishment, he laughs. It's more of a chuckle than a full-on belly laugh, but still. I didn't know he could do that.

"Very prettily said. Well, you have my cell number if you run into any problems. This will be a good experience for you, socializing with important people in a casual environment. If your research takes off the way it looks like it's going to, you're going to need to meet a lot of wealthy and influential people."

Bile threatens to choke me. "I… will?"

He nods. "I'm afraid so. Rich people like to think they're being philanthropic by funding scientific research, but they make sure they get every ounce of recognition they can from it. Including having scientists fawn all over them."

That sounds… fun. I muster up a weak smile. "Yay."

He chuckles again. "One thing I'm not clear on is

how David Carew heard about your research in the first place."

"Oh. He, uh, found out about it because he knows one of the participants. A dragon." That's not a lie. It just leaves out part of the story.

The director nods again. "One of the dragons who visited you the other week?"

How…?

"Yes." I rack my brain, trying to think of a reason he would know about that.

"I think that might have been the first time a dragon was ever in this building," he muses. "Chris says they were quite enthusiastic."

"I don't have a lot of experience with dragons," I reply honestly, "but that seems to be their default setting."

He seems to be deep in thought about something, and I wonder if he's done with me. This is the longest one-on-one meeting I've had with him since he interviewed me to work here.

He clears his throat. "Chris seemed to think one of them was particularly enthusiastic about you."

I blink a few times. Is he saying…? Panic grips me so tightly, I feel like I can't breathe. "Sir, I would never—"

He holds up a hand. "I'm not questioning your ethics, Dr. Griffiths. In fact, given the nature of your research, I don't believe there could be any cause to call your ethics into question even if one of your participants was… overly enthusiastic about you."

That's a euphemism I've never heard before.

"Uh, sir—"

"All I'm saying," he interrupts again, "is that if you were so inclined, it wouldn't cause any trouble."

This is too weird. "Understood, sir." I don't really understand, but I figure Sura will, and that way I don't have to continue having this uncomfortable conversation with my boss.

His face takes on a politely dismissive expression. "I'll keep an eye out for the email with your plan," he says, and I smile and agree and get up.

"Thank you, sir."

When I close the door behind me, his assistant glances at me, clearly wondering why I'm still polluting her space. I'm not sure what takes over me, but I grin cheekily at her and say, "I hope you're having a great day!"

The weight of her astonished stare follows me out into the hallway.

Sura is waiting impatiently for me, though she's pretending to work. I can tell she's only pretending because she's staring thoughtfully at the screen, as though concentrating. If she was actually working, she'd be scowling at it and tapping a pen or her fingers or her foot. Sura is not a quiet worker.

"Well?" she demands.

I fill her in. "So what did he mean?" I ask impatiently, and she shakes her head at me in disbelief.

"You need to get out of the lab more."

"Sura." I try not to whine.

"He was telling you to do whatever it takes to keep the dragons happy."

My jaw drops. "No way."

She smiles smugly.

"He's pimping me out?" My voice rises on the last word, and she smacks my arm.

"Of course he's not. If you don't want to, nobody's

going to force you. But if you did want to, and Fabian—I assume that's who he was talking about—would be happy about it, and say nice things about you and KRD to the wing leader, then…" She shrugs, as though it makes sense for me to fuck someone to make my boss happy.

I don't know what to say.

"How did he know Fabian wants you, anyway?"

I blink away my buzzing thoughts. "He said Chris mentioned it."

"Receptionist Chris? How would he know? I thought Fabian only came on to you when you two were alone."

It's my turn to shrug. "Maybe he mentioned it to Dustin while they were walking out. You know Chris's hearing is phenomenal."

Sura's frowning, but she seems to accept that. "Anyway," she continues, "I guess that's not important. You have other priorities right now."

"Like putting together a plan to expand my research." This is going to be so epic.

"No. Well, yes. But first, you need to buy some decent clothes for this weekend, including sexy underwear."

"I can't talk to you when you're like this." I turn on my heel and take the three steps to my desk, but she's up and following me before I get there.

"No, hear me out. I'm being genuine. Your closet is full of work clothes, right? Chinos and shirts and one good suit. Do you even own jeans anymore?"

"Of course I own jeans!" Although… now that she mentions it… "They might be a bit too worn for this weekend." There are holes. And not the strategic designer kind. I have another pair, but they don't fit anymore. I also bought them in the 1990s, and I think styles have changed since then.

"That's what I thought. So we go shopping, get you some casual but classy clothes to wear to the home of the dragon wing leader, where you will meet all kinds of people you need to impress."

"I think I'm going to throw up."

She pats my shoulder. "You'll be fine. The clothes will give your confidence a boost. And you could talk about your research in your sleep, remember."

Tell that to my suddenly shaking hands.

"And new underwear because you haven't had sex in too long and need your pipes cleaned, and now that the director has essentially given you the green light, there's nothing to stop you and Fabian from doing it dragon-style." She pauses. "I don't know what that is, but you can tell me all about it on Monday."

Slowly, I look up at her fake-innocent expression. "We can no longer be friends."

CHAPTER FIVE

Fabian

ON FRIDAY AFTERNOON, Brandt and Percy come home early from the city, right around midafternoon. I'm only just home from college myself. It's easier now that I don't have to wait for Dustin to finish his classes. I can just come and go as I please. The only problem is that sometimes I get distracted while I'm driving, since there's nobody in the car with me to keep me focused, and I already got two tickets this week. But I also had a date with the deputy who gave them to me on Wednesday night. He was nice but seemed confused a lot. I don't think we'll go out again. He did wave at me when I drove past today, though.

"Why are they home early?" I ask Kethe, peering out the kitchen window down the length of the back lawn, where Brandt and Steffen have just shifted back to their biped form and Percy is gathering up the harness.

"Probably so they can be ready when our guests arrive," she answers, not looking up from where she's icing a cake. It looks delicious—Kethe loves YouTube and has become obsessed with fancy cake decorating.

For reasons I don't fully understand, cakes with pretty decorations make my mouth water more than the plainly iced ones. Wil has a theory that it's because our brains see all the frosting and automatically calculate how good the extra sugar will taste. Steffen thinks it's a conspiracy between the baking industry and pharmaceutical companies to increase the number of humans who'll become insulin dependent. I'm pretty sure it doesn't work that way, but it's one of his more believable conspiracy theories.

Whatever the reason, I already tried to sneak some frosting and had my fingers rapped with the wooden spoon.

"Are there people coming today? I thought they were all arriving tomorrow." Although that does explain the cake. She normally doesn't go to so much trouble when it's just going to be us—not unless she's practicing a new technique.

She sighs and shoots me an exasperated glance. "Have you not been listening at all this week?"

"To what?" I turn away from the window and give her my full attention. Well… most of it. A tiny bit is wondering if I can sneak one of those fun-size Snickers bars away while she's not watching.

"To everything that's been discussed. David and Caolan are coming tonight, and so is the scientist who's going to be working with Sophie and the others."

I frown. "Working with them on what?"

Shaking her head, Kethe says, "Honestly, Fabian, I don't know how you manage to get through every day. You remember Sophie and Brandt asking you to search your records to see if there had been any lessening in dragon magic over the past few thousand years?"

"Of course," I declare indignantly. I never forget a records search. "But there wasn't any. I checked three times, and our magic use and capacity is consistent with records going back almost to the beginning." I'm so offended that she thinks I forgot that I decide to risk the Snickers grab.

"Yes, but the reason they asked—which they told you at the time—was because the other species have all seen a downturn in their capacity to use their abilities." She lashes out with the spatula in her hand, smacking my fingers again as they creep toward the chocolate. I jerk my hand back and pout. Joke's on her, though—the spatula had frosting on it, so now I get to lick that off my fingers.

My bruised, stinging fingers.

It's worth it.

"I won't tell you again," she warns. "Next time, there'll be no cookies or desserts for a week."

"Fiiiiine," I say, then smirk and lick my hand. She rolls her eyes. "So there's a scientist who's going to help find out why that's happening?" That sounds interesting. I wonder why I don't remember them talking about it.

"No, Fabian," Brandt says from the doorway, and I turn to look at him. Percy pushes past him and heads directly for the cupboard where the tea is stored. "Dr. Griffiths's research will help us assess the breadth of the issue and hopefully to improve things, but it's unlikely to be able to identify the cause."

"Dr. Griffiths? *My* Dr. Griffiths?"

Brandt raises a brow as he takes a seat at the kitchen table. "Is he yours?"

"I was the one who found him." There's a sulky note in my voice I don't fully understand. "The least you could have done was mention that you were going to be working with him."

"I'm not," Brandt says. "Not much, anyway. Sophie will be."

"And we did mention it," Percy reminds me, joining Brandt with two steaming mugs. "We discussed it last weekend and then specifically came home on Tuesday night so we could work out the details of the extra people who'd be coming this weekend. You were at the table when we talked about it. You even contributed to the conversation."

"I did?" I don't remember discussing this on Tuesday. Surely I wouldn't have forgotten something this important.

"This cake was your idea," Kethe adds. "I was going to make a triple chocolate one, and you suggested Snickers instead."

Ohhhhhh. That, I remember. "I suggested it because Snickers is Caolan's favorite. You didn't say Dr. Rhys was coming too."

"Dr. Rhys?" Steffen asks sharply as he enters. "Who's that? Their name isn't on my list."

"It's Dr. Griffiths," Percy reassures him. "For reasons he's about to tell us, Fabian calls him Dr. Rhys."

"It's less formal but still encompasses all his achievements," I explain. "So he's coming tonight? I invited him to come tomorrow, but that was before you all began plotting things without telling me."

"Plots? What plots?" Steffen stares at me as though trying to see into my brain. Who knows, maybe he actually can. As a species, we've evolved over time to be able to fulfil our own needs. Maybe Steffen has such a need to know whether people are conspiring that he's evolved a way to be able to read minds.

Hmm. That's probably something I, as record keeper, should be aware of. Maybe I need to test the theory. I return Stef's stare and *think* as hard as I can in his direction. *"Can you hear me?"*

"Fabian, are you okay? You look like you're constipated." Kethe studies me. "Do you need some of that licorice tea? It'll loosen things up for you."

"I'm fine," I assure her. "I was just thinking." I glance over at Steffen, but he gives no indication that he might have heard my attempt to make contact. I guess that doesn't prove anything, but I can likely put the possibility of him being able to read minds on the back burner.

I'm disappointed. That would have been fun.

But in the meantime, Dr. Rhys is coming to stay for the weekend!

"I'm still waiting for someone to tell me about the plots," Steffen demands. "Do I need to get the emergency response kits out?"

"There are no plots," Percy says firmly. "Fabian, tell him there are no plots."

"It was a figure of speech," I tell Steffen, mostly because the emergency response plan requires us to wear gas masks, and those things are so uncomfortable. No matter how often Sophie explains to Stef that the poisonous gases on this planet don't affect dragons that way, he insists we be on guard. "But I do think someone could have mentioned he was coming early."

"Do you have a special interest in *Dr. Rhys* that you want to tell us about?" Brandt asks slyly.

I shrug. "As the person who discovered him and his

work, I think it would have been good manners for you to keep me in the loop. And I want to fuck him, but he's worried about ethics. These Earth species have managed to turn sex into a complicated ethical conundrum."

"Thank you." Percy's voice is bone dry. "I feel I should note here that sex *is* a complicated ethical conundrum."

"Not when you have two freely consenting adults. Then it should just be fun." I smile dreamily as I think about all the fun Dr. Rhys and I could have together. "He's awfully muscular."

"Later you can tell us all how you know that." Kethe hands me the empty frosting bowl and the spatula, and I immediately begin scraping it clean and eating the last remnants of delicious caramel buttercream. "But before then, let this be your reminder that you will respect Dr. Griffiths's boundaries or you'll answer to me."

I almost drop the spatula in surprise. "I would never violate his boundaries! Not unless we were role playing and it was all agreed beforehand, anyway." That could be a lot of fun. "I already told him I'd wait until he's got rid of his ethics for us to have sex."

Percy briefly closes his eyes and sighs. "Of course you did. Tell me, did you use those exact words?"

Pursing my lips, I think about it. "Maybe? Or maybe not. Once he said we couldn't have sex right away, I was more focused on my questions about Welsh culture."

To my surprise, Kethe laughs and leans in to kiss my cheek. "Oh, Fabian. Never change."

"I wasn't planning to, but thank you. It's always nice to be appreciated."

"Do we have any of that shifter whiskey left?" Percy asks, apropos of nothing.

WHEN I TRACKED down Sophie and grilled her for details, she told me Dr. Rhys planned to arrive by six. She also gave me a list of information she needed from the living archive, but none of it is urgent, so I put it on my desk and went down to wait for Dr. Rhys to arrive. I plan to keep my promise to respect his boundaries—nothing is sexy about a man who feels pressured—but there's no harm in reminding him that I'm here and waiting anytime he's ready.

Steffen's already in the great hall, pacing up and down beside the hearth and muttering to himself.

"What are you doing?" I ask, and he whirls on me and glares.

"Waiting for this scientist." He manages to make "scientist" sound like "serial killing cannibal."

"Why?" Is it just me, or is Steffen getting more tense lately? When was the last time he had a good fuck?

Actually… does Steffen fuck? Could he ever relax enough to let someone that close?

Sorrow rises to swamp me. Imagine being so afraid of the universe that you never let anyone just be with you. Impulsively, I step up to him and wrap my arms around his torso, holding tight.

He throws me across the room, and I slam into the wall with a resounding crash, then slide down it to sprawl on the floor.

"*Owwww.*"

The sound of running footsteps echoes through the house as everyone converges on the great hall, and Steffen stalks across the space between us, looming over me, his magic coursing strongly through him.

"What's going on here?" Brandt's voice booms, magnified by his magic and the weight of his power as wing leader. "Steffen, stand down now!"

"It's fine," I gasp, trying to drag myself mostly to a sitting position. Sophie and Percy hurry over to help me. "It's fine. Steffen misunderstood."

"You attacked me," Stef says, but he sounds uncertain, and he hasn't reached for his magic again.

"I hugged you," I correct, wincing as Sophie prods my ribs. Something's cracked there.

"What?" The question comes from multiple mouths.

"This is my fault," I add. "I know better than to touch Stef without warning. And it was a tight hug. I'm sorry I startled you, but I swear it wasn't an attack. I wouldn't attack you. You're my friend."

"I am?"

Ouch. "I thought you were." As much as he has friends, anyway. And that just makes me want to hug him again, even though Sophie still hasn't healed the injuries from the last hug.

The lost look on his face is heartbreaking, and it occurs to me that maybe I haven't been paying enough attention to the people close to me lately. I've been focused on the records and learning new things and getting off, but records aren't any good if the people they represent are falling apart.

"Okay," Brandt says calmly. "Fabian, don't do that again. Let's respect Steffen's boundaries."

"I will. I'm sorry," I say to Steffen, but if anything, that makes him look even more forlorn.

"Steffen, there's nobody here who will attack you. You know that, right?" Brandt finally releases his magic and comes closer, reaching out a hand to Stef, who looks at it blankly. "Let's go take a break."

That stirs something of the normal Steffen back to life. "There's a stranger coming," he protests.

"It's okay, Stef." Wil comes through the doorway. "I've just checked the security system, and everything's online. David and Caolan came through a portal a minute ago. Between us, we can handle anything that might happen. You ran a check on Dr. Griffiths and found nothing to worry about, remember?"

"You can never be too careful," he frets but then nods. "Don't let him wander through the house until you've got his measure, though."

"I swear I won't," Wil assures him. "I trust your judgment."

Steffen hesitates a moment longer, then follows Brandt out of the great hall. We all listen in silence as they walk toward Brandt's office, go in, and then there's a complete lack of noise that indicates a privacy shield.

Kethe lets out a huge sigh. "That poor boy. It's starting to take over."

"I didn't realize it had gotten so bad," Sophie admits, still poking me in various places, although by this point, I think she's doing it for sadistic pleasure. "He's always been paranoid, but to strike at one of us…"

"It's my fault," I reiterate firmly. I don't want any of them blaming Stef. "But I do think he's getting worse. Is he even close to anyone outside of us?"

We all look at Wil, who knows Steffen the best. He bites his lip, then shakes his head.

"He keeps most people at a distance. I try to spend time with him outside of work, but…"

Kethe puts an arm around him. "We'll do more," she promises. "He needs to feel safe and loved here."

Before Wil can reply, we hear David and Caolan coming in through the sunroom door, and the gate buzzer sounds.

"Shit," Wil says, glancing at where I'm still sitting on the floor.

"Let him in," Percy says calmly. "Sophie, will Fabian survive?"

"Can anyone really be sure?" she muses as Wil moves toward the door. "His brain is a complex and annoying thing. But he's not seriously injured, and I can heal his breaks and bruises."

"Hello?" a voice calls down the hallway. "Where is everyone?"

"We're here, David," Percy shouts back.

Wil hits the button on the panel for the microphone. "Hello?"

My ears are sharp enough to hear Dr. Rhys's words. "Hi. I, um, was invited? I'm Rhys Griffiths." I crane my neck, trying to see his face on the little screen, but my and Wil's current positions make it impossible. Just as well, because moving my neck like that makes my head hurt something fierce.

"Come on through, Dr. Griffiths. Just follow the drive." Wil presses the button to open the gates, then steps back from the security panel.

"Whoaaaa," David says as he and Caolan come through the doorway and sees me half sprawled on the floor with the others crouched around me. "What happened here?" His gaze darts around, making a security assessment, and I remember that he's a combat sorcerer. Caolan's elf magic rises, but Percy gets to his feet and motions them to calm.

"It's fine. There was a misunderstanding."

Caolan's eyes go to the wall behind me. "That looks like a big misunderstanding."

I twist around to see what he means but stop with a cry. That fucking hurt!

"Stay still," Sophie scolds. "I'll heal you now." She puts her hands on me, and I feel the familiar, soothing brush of her magic. Sophie is not a soothing person generally, so her magic always surprises me. It funnels through my body, touching every cell, and the pain fades away.

She sits back on her heels. "There. Now stop doing stupid things."

I move my head cautiously, but it doesn't hurt. "I will," I assure her, then turn around to see why Percy, Caolan, and Kethe are staring at the wall and muttering to each other.

The answer is that there's a Fabian-sized dent in it. "Wow. No wonder I hurt so much. You can actually see the outline of my body."

"Not something to brag about," Wil calls over his shoulder as he and David open the front door and go out, presumably to meet Dr. Rhys. I try to scramble up and follow them, but Sophie grabs my arm in an iron grip and hauls me back down. "What?" I whine.

"You've been impetuous enough for one day. Sit here and think over your decisions."

I squint at her. "Are you mad at me?"

She huffs and rolls her eyes. "Am I mad? Of course I'm fucking mad, Fabian! You walk through life without paying any attention to what's going on around you. It's a miracle that you've survived this long, but all your close calls—which, fine, I laughed about, but none of them have made you wake up and see that you need to be a little more careful. Just this week, you got pulled over for reckless driving, and it wasn't even deliberate! That's a danger not just to you, but to everyone else on the road with you *and* to our entire species and the community if the humans pay too much attention to you."

Right now, I'm really glad I didn't tell anyone about the second time I was pulled over.

"I'd never do it on purpose," I protest, and she closes her eyes briefly.

"That's part of the problem. You're not paying attention, and things go wrong. You get excited about bondage with some random person you picked up and end up cuffed to a pipe in their basement for two days. You signed up for a science experiment without knowing it because you weren't listening. What if that ring wasn't just a monitor? What if it affected your brain or body? You know Steffen is paranoid, but you put your arms around him without warning. If you'd hit the wall at a slightly different angle, there might not have been anything for me to heal, Fabian. I can't bring you back from death. And you can't continue wandering through life without considering the consequences of your decisions or even paying attention to the decisions you're making."

I swallow. Am I really that bad?

The great hall is silent, and I glance away from Sophie to where the others are. They're watching me solemnly.

"We love you, Fabian," Kethe says softly. "We don't

want to lose you because you didn't think things through. Just try to pay a bit more attention."

I nod. "I can do that." I look back at Sophie. "I can do that."

Her smile is sad. "I know you can. I'm sorry I yelled."

"I'm sorry you had to." I mean it. I don't ever want to be the reason my family is suffering.

We all hear the car pull up outside, and Sophie draws back enough for me to get up. I glance at the wall. "Should we fix that?"

Percy studies it, then shakes his head. "Leave it."

Intriguing. I wonder what kind of impression he wants to make?

Outside, David's greeting Dr. Rhys and introducing Wil. "Brandt was called into a meeting just a moment ago, but Fabian's inside… and Percy. Have you met Percy yet?"

"Not yet," Dr. Rhys replies. "It would be an honor."

Aww, that's sweet. I forget sometimes that Percy used to lead the community government. He's just our Percy now, who looks after us and stops us from making big mistakes.

They come inside, and Dr. Rhys's eyes widen the way everyone's do when they first see the great hall. It's kind of spectacular, with the massive fireplace and the four-floors-high soaring ceiling with a giant chandelier among the rafters. Then his gaze lands on the damaged wall and narrows slightly.

"Hi, Dr. Rhys!" I walk forward with my hand extended. I'd like to give him a hug, see if he's muscular all over, but I'm respecting his boundaries. Besides, he's dressed a little more casually today, in nice jeans and a short-sleeved polo shirt, and I can see that he definitely is.

"Hello, Fabian. It's nice to see you again." His voice is steady and polite but not warm. That's okay. I have time to make him like me.

"This is Percy Caraway," I introduce, doing my best to make him feel comfortable and welcome. I can take social cues when I'm paying attention.

"Welcome to Here Be Dragons," Percy says warmly, taking Dr. Rhys's hand. "It's lovely to meet you. I've been hearing a lot about your research."

As Percy puts our guest at ease, I hear another car coming up the driveway. It has to be Dustin and his professor, since nobody buzzed at the gate and we're expecting them anyway. And sure enough, a minute later, car doors slam and I hear Dustin complaining about the driveway being blocked. He bounds up the stairs and through the still-open front door.

"Hey! Why's there a car— What the fuck happened here?" He stares at the dent in the plaster with his mouth open.

"Good evening," Rob, Dustin's *much* better half, says to Dr. Rhys. "We haven't met. I'm Rob Sarris."

"Rhys Griffiths."

"Ah, the source of Fabian's purity ring. Dustin's told me about you. Would you be interested in having a human in your study? I know we don't have magic, but—"

"I think that sounds like an excellent idea," Sophie says.

"You do?" Dr. Rhys sounds doubtful, and I jump in to prove my worth.

"It really is. And humans do— Ow!" I jerk away from Sophie's pointy elbow.

"Sorry," she says innocently. "Muscle spasm. As Fabian was saying, humans do share a lot of physical and mental similarities with the community species, so it couldn't hurt to have some human participants. A control group of sorts."

Dr. Rhys looks at her like she just sprouted a second head. I tried doing that once out of curiosity. It wasn't fun. "That's not how control groups work. But if you think having some humans in the study is a good idea, I guess it can't hurt. Maybe one day you'll explain exactly why."

"All things come one day," Sophie agrees serenely. I move out of reach, just in case.

"Anyway," Percy says, just a touch louder than necessary, "there's no reason for us all to be standing around with the door open. Dr. Griffiths, if you'll give your keys to Wil, he'll park your car for you while Kethe shows you up to your room. Dinner is in…" He glances at Kethe, who checks her watch.

"About forty-five minutes. But we'll have drinks he— er, in the sunroom, whenever you're ready."

Usually when we have guests, pre-dinner drinks are here in the great hall, so it's not hard to guess why Kethe hesitated.

"That sounds great." Dr. Rhys smiles somewhat reticently. "I can move my car, though. I don't want to put anyone out."

"Not putting me out at all," Will declares, and Dr. Rhys hands over his keys.

Dustin waits until the sound of Dr. Rhys's and

Kethe's steps fades completely before rounding on us. "What's *that* about?" He points to the wall.

"Steffen threw Fabian into it," Wil says calmly. "Rob, did you want to move your car too?"

Rob, who is possibly the calmest person ever born, since he thinks Dustin is cute, smiles. "Sure."

"Steffen *threw* Fabian?" Dustin ignores the wave his boyfriend gives as he departs and the door closes, instead looking me up and down. "Why?"

"I'm fine, by the way. Sophie healed me. Then tried to poke a hole in my side." I glare at her.

She glares right back. "Human magic isn't widely known, remember? Most members of the community have no idea it's possible."

Oh. I'd forgotten that. CSG didn't want to cause widespread fear, so it's been kept under wraps except for some of the older mixed-species couples, where the human needs to learn magic to extend their lifespan. "Oops?"

"We *just* finished talking about this," she lectures. "You need to pay attention and think things through."

Percy clears his throat. "Okay, Sophie. I'm sure Fabian's sorry, and there was no harm done. Let's move on."

"Hello!" Dustin shouts. "We can't move on until someone tells me why Steffen threw Fabian at the wall!"

"I hugged him."

Dustin folds his arms and glares at me. "Fine. Don't tell me, then."

"It's true," Percy confirms, and for the second time since he arrived, Dustin gapes.

"I can't leave you alone for a second," he breathes, shaking his head at me.

I'm getting tired of this. I'm not *that* bad. Not like

Achatius, a dragon who lived two or three hundred thousand cycles ago, who was so disconnected from the world around him that he once walked right through an elven battlefield, aimlessly dodging magical and physical attacks, without noticing what it was. I'd notice if someone came at me with an ax or if a fireball exploded inches away.

He was a truly fascinating dragon, though, who posited and then proved a number of theories that changed our world. He also wrote some papers about his time here on Earth and the things he'd have liked to try implementing here if he ever came back. I wonder if he ever did? If not, some of those theories might be worth looking into.

Starting toward the hallway, I'm intent on searching the living archive for all the information we have on Achatius, but a hand grabs my arm. I blink at Dustin.

"If you're done proving our point," Sophie says grimly, "let's go get something to drink."

Proving their… oh. Yeah. I did fade right out of that conversation, didn't I?

I can do better.

"We're really not going to fix the wall?" I ask, trying to sound like that's what I was thinking all along.

"Not just yet." Percy glances up at the damage again. "Let's see what Brandt thinks."

Great. Another person who needs to be reminded that I can't be left alone.

CHAPTER SIX

Rhys

Dinner's not exactly weird, but it feels like it wants to be. There's this odd undercurrent that I don't know what to do with. Nobody's talking about the giant hole in the wall in the entrance room. Fabian appears to be on his best behavior… or at least, he's not the airy, alternately vague and hyperfocused dragon I met previously. I even made a deliberate reference to calling my mom in Wales, and though his face lit up and he opened his mouth like he had questions, he said nothing and just smiled. The smile was a bit forced, but it still made him too attractive for words.

And I think something's going on with Steffen, who was introduced to me as Brandt's head of security. Everyone's being very gentle with him. Maybe he's had bad news or a recent loss or something, because surely the head of security wouldn't need to be babied all the time?

The conversation is congenial and interesting, and I get a lot of questions about my research that are insightful enough to indicate actual engagement, but I just can't shake the feeling that something is off.

The main course is cleared, and conversation turns to the gathering tomorrow. Apparently, its purpose is to introduce Rob to more dragons now that he and Dustin are officially together. There's a story there, but honestly, I'm not sure if I'm brave enough to ask. These dragons are lovely, but in the way a kitten high on catnip is lovely.

"…excited to introduce you to more of my friends," Dustin is saying to Rob, patting his arm. Rob looks somewhat less excited by the prospect of meeting all Dustin's friends, but the smile he gives the blond man speaks very clearly of why he's doing it anyway. I've never seen so much love in a single look.

I clear my throat, feeling like I'm intruding somehow, even though there are nearly a dozen of us here and there's no expectation of privacy. Fortunately, Kethe chooses that moment to come back into the dining room carrying a tall, gorgeous-looking cake. Wil follows her with a stack of plates.

"Wow," David says. "We really should eat here more often. No wonder Percy's always so keen to get home for the weekend."

"You're such a good boy," Kethe says fondly, depositing the cake on the table. "You're welcome here anytime."

"Are those baby Snickers bars on top?" Caolan asks, leaning forward eagerly.

"Yes. It's a Snickers cake." Kethe sounds smug, and I learn why when Caolan hops out of his chair and circles the table to hug her.

"I've always liked you, Kethe, even before Brandt and Percy got together and I really got to know you."

I join the laughter and add my compliment to everyone else's. The cake looks divine, and even though I would have sworn I was too full to eat more, my mouth is now watering for a slice.

I'm nearly done with the rich chocolate-peanut-butter cake, soft nougat filling, and caramel butter-cream, when I happen to glance across the table and see Fabian licking that same caramel buttercream off a spoon, his pink tongue swiping up every last bit. My cock stirs with interest, and I try to make myself look away. I'm in a room full of shifters. If I get aroused, they'll smell it, and while I'm sure they're too good-mannered to mention it, we'll all know what happened. I don't need to seem unprofessional, even if the director did all but give me permission to go forth and fuck.

But for some reason, I can't tear my eyes away.

And then… it gets worse.

Fabian glances down at his plate, where the only thing remaining is a small glob of icing, then casually swipes his finger through it and lifts it to his mouth. Time seems to drag out, and I watch in slow motion as his tongue comes out again, wrapping around the finger he sucks between his puffy pink lips.

I make a strangled sound and shoot to my feet. "Uh, where's the restroom?"

With a concerned frown, Percy gives me directions, and I leave as quickly as I can without looking like I'm running. Which I am. Running away. From a man I don't think I can resist.

In the charming half bath, I run my wrists under

cold water and chant affirmations while staring at myself in the mirror. Sura read a book about it once.

"I am in control of my body. My career is more important than sex. I don't find him that attractive."

It doesn't work. An image of Fabian licking frosting off his finger rises in my mind's eye, and I groan. I'd learn how to fucking bake if it meant having him lick frosting off me that way.

Sighing, I turn off the water and dry my hands, then look myself dead in the eye. "Don't let this fuck things up for you. But if you really want him…" I swallow. "… go for it."

I can't believe I just said that. Or that I now have to rejoin the group knowing that I've given myself permission to hook up with Fabian and my cock is still half hard.

Why me?

Back in the dining room, coffee and chocolates are being passed around. I slide into my seat and smile my thanks at Kethe. "I can't remember the last time I ate so well," I comment, then want to kick myself. It's not the best remark to make after fleeing to the bathroom.

Fortunately, nobody says anything, although Dustin does snicker softly.

I forge ahead. "I'd love a short walk after dinner. Maybe Fabian could give me a tour of the grounds?" I'm not sure if dragons can hear as well as other shifters, but hopefully that will give us enough distance to talk. I could always weave a privacy ward, but that might seem rude, since I'm a guest here.

"A tour? Alone? Just us? What an excellent idea!"

Okay then. I wasn't subtle, but Fabian takes it to extremes.

"I think I feel like a walk too. I'll join you," Dustin says innocently.

"No, you won't. You have that thing to do." Fabian glares at him.

"Thing? What thing? There's no thing."

Rob leans over and whispers something to him, and Dustin's face goes pink.

"Ohhhhh, that thing. Yes, I have to do that. A lot. In fact, let's go do that thing right now. Fabian, you should do the thing too."

I think I might die of embarrassment. Lucky for me, nearly everyone is focused on Rob and Dustin, who look only slightly flustered as they wish us all a good evening and leave in the face of suggestive leers. I think Sophie wanted to say something, but then she looked at me and didn't. Maybe I'm not the only one trying to appear professional tonight.

"Let's take that walk," Fabian suggests brightly, but Brandt laughs.

"Rhys has to finish his coffee first," he chides. There's a wicked gleam to his eyes that makes me think he's deliberately torturing Fabian, who sighs and subsides in his chair.

"You shouldn't walk alone with a stranger this late," Steffen says suddenly. "It's twilight already and will be dark soon."

I'm not sure why, but it seems like the whole room collectively relaxes.

"Dr. Rhys isn't a stranger," Fabian says, aiming for cheerful, but just a hair off. There's definitely something going on here that I'm missing. "And we won't be out there long."

Steffen's jaw sets. "But the grounds are large. It will

take a while to show him around. And he might not be a stranger, but he's…" He trails off when Percy nudges him.

"It's fine, Stef. I don't think they're going to tour the whole grounds."

"Or any of them," Fabian adds. "I was planning to go right to that corner that's out of sight of all the windows… so we can 'talk.'"

My face flames. Yep, he definitely doesn't get the point of subtlety.

David grins at me. "I'd be sympathetic, but this is really nothing compared to what I went through."

"Hey!" Caolan exclaims indignantly.

I toss back the last of my coffee. This is only going to keep getting worse the longer I delay. "I'm ready. Kethe, can I help you clear?"

She waves me off. "No, there are plenty of hands to help. Enjoy your walk." Her voice trembles slightly on the last word.

I don't think I'm ever going to live this down. Thank fuck Sura's not here.

Fabian's already on his feet and watching me impatiently, so I push back from the table and excuse myself. It's not until we get outside that he says anything, and it's not what I expect.

"We're not actually going to that corner. Stef has about thirty cameras pointing at it, and everyone's probably racing to the surveillance room right this second."

"Oh." It sounds faint, but I can't manage anything else. Lovely. Cameras. To watch us… whatever. So glad we didn't go there.

"This way." He leads me across the terrace and off the side, then into some trees. "Stef has cameras set up here too, and some of the windows have a pretty good view, but there's one tree… that one." He grabs my hand and tugs me behind a huge oak. "This is a blind spot."

"It's not a security risk, is it?" I don't know why I ask that. It just seems relevant?

Fabian shakes his head. "Nope. A step in any direction and you're out of it. Someone would have to open a portal to this exact spot and then not move at all. It would be easier to fire a missile at the house."

"What a charming thought."

He laughs. "That's exactly what Percy said when Stef explained. But don't worry, there's an anti-missile alert system or something like that. Steffen's always prepared for anything."

I hesitate, feeling like I should ask but not sure how. "Is he… um, he seemed more reserved than the rest of you tonight."

Fabian's mouth turns down at the corners. "He's had a bad day. But we didn't come out here to talk about Steffen." He stops suddenly. "You didn't really want a tour, did you?"

I snort. "What would you do if I said yes?"

He shrugs, but he's frowning now. "Give you a tour. I'm all about respecting boundaries."

I lean against the tree trunk and smile at him. "There's no boundary." I almost expect him to jump on me, but instead he just smiles back and leans in to lightly drum his fingertips against my chest. The rings on his fingers glimmer in the fading light.

"What changed your mind?"

I didn't think he'd moved closer, but somehow he's near enough that I can feel the heat from his body. And there's a lot of it. If he moves even the tiniest bit, we'll be pressed up against each other, and I want that. Desperately.

But he asked me a question. "It was pointed out to me by several people that I was being overly strict with my application of ethical standards." I cringe. That sentence was ridiculously pompous. "And I want to fuck you," I blurt, trying to make up for it and instead managing to sound like I'm trying too hard. I remember now why giving up dating wasn't that big of a deal. It's hard work.

However, I like sex, and if I want to have more of it —and have it with Fabian—I need to get through this part.

"What if I want to fuck you?" he asks solemnly. My cock goes from half hard to fully erect and ready for action.

"Yes. That sounds good."

The sentence is barely out of my mouth before his lips are on mine.

I fall into the sensation of warm mouth on mouth, mingling breath. Fabian dots tiny kisses at the corners of my lips before swooping back in to claim me in a kiss so deep, I think I might drown in it. He presses me to the tree and owns my mouth, and all I can do is give myself up to him and hope it never ends.

Eventually, I break the kiss. It takes an effort, because kissing Fabian is like a feast for a starving man.

"What?" he mutters, chasing after me.

"I want you in me."

His eyes widen. "Yessss," he hisses, then looks around, and I know he's thinking about the blind spot. Unless we want to risk being seen, our options here are severely limited. Which might be fun to try one day, but right now, I want to be able to explore every inch of his skin and not have to worry about my dick getting tree bark grazes while he pounds into me from behind. "We have to go inside."

I nod. "Okay."

He straightens my collar, pats his hair, then says, "Come on." I find it stupidly endearing that he tidied us up, as though anyone we run into won't immediately know what we've been up to and what we're going to do.

We walk back through the trees, across the terrace, and sneak in through the sunroom. By this point, Fabian is tiptoeing, which makes me want to laugh. I bite my lip to choke the sound back, then follow him to a small staircase near the back of the house. We go up two floors without seeing anyone, then sneak down a hallway, only for Fabian to jerk me to a halt when a door opens and Caolan steps out.

He takes one look at us and grins. "Nice tour?"

"Lovely, thanks," I manage. "Fabian was just showing me back to my room. This place is like a maze."

Caolan just laughs. Fabian tugs at my sleeve. "Come *on*, we're wasting time. I knew this would happen if someone saw us!"

I manage a "Bye" to Caolan before Fabian yanks me past him. I guess I misunderstood the reason for his sneaking. He's not worried about people seeing us; he just doesn't want to get delayed by them.

We make it to my room, and Fabian throws open the door with relief. "I thought you'd be more comfortable here," he suggests. "We can even use your lube, if you like."

My face gets hot. I did bring lube, which usually isn't something I'd pack for a visit to a patron's home. But Sura's shopping trip and the director's comments got me thinking that it wasn't a terrible idea to be prepared, and it's not like lube will go to waste. I can always use it by myself.

Speaking of Sura's shopping trip…

I close the door behind us. "I have to warn you, my friend took me shopping for some new clothes and she got a bit carried away."

He blinks at me. "I don't understand. Are we… I thought you wanted to have sex?"

"I do," I assure him.

"Is this a custom I don't know about? Something unique to the Welsh? Do you need me to do a wardrobe inspection? Or a raid! I've been fascinated by the concept of a panty raid. Is that what this is?" He looks around so eagerly, I'm reluctant to disappoint him.

"No, sorry. I might have made too big a deal of this. There's no custom or anything. It's just… she suggested I buy sexy underwear. So… I don't want you thinking this is what I usually wear or anything." Although… would it really have mattered if he did think that? What's the big deal? Now I've made this into a thing, whereas if I'd said nothing, he might not even have noticed. They're not that sexy. There's no sequins or whatever.

Do people who aren't stripping wear sequined underwear?

I'm pondering that when Fabian grabs my waistband and starts opening my jeans. "I want to see," he insists.

"It's really not that interesting," I protest, wishing I'd

just shut up in the first place, but he already has my zipper down, so I kick off my shoes and stand there obediently as he shoves my pants to the floor.

Then whistles through his teeth. "You *do* work out. Take off your shirt."

Flattered but also feeling vaguely objectified—and weirdly turned on by that—I pull my polo over my head and drop it to the floor as I step out of my pants.

Fabian takes a deep breath and sighs, his gaze running over my body like a caress. "Oh, yes," he murmurs. "Turn around."

Completely self-conscious, I turn in a circle. I know I'm in good shape—working out is part of my routine and helps wake my brain up every morning—but he's acting like I've got the abs of an underwear model.

A hand grabs my ass, and I jump.

"I like how high they're cut," he says with a light squeeze. I shiver. "This is fun. Did you buy any others? Maybe we should have a fashion show."

Uhhh, no. Determined to get things back on track, I step away from him and turn around. My cock strains against my briefs. It knows what it wants. Fabian's gaze drops to take it in.

"On the other hand," he concedes, "we have other things to do right now." He strips off his clothes faster than I would've thought possible, leaving me to admire the smooth, sleek skin and muscle exposed. He's toned all over, but not muscular, and my fingers itch to touch.

My gaze trails down his chest, over his stomach. I force myself to go slow, to make my first glimpse of his cock a big reveal. It's stupid, but it feels more special that way.

Finally I reach his groin, and—

What. The. Fuck.

I shouldn't be this surprised. Most species have different-shaped cocks. I don't know why I was expecting dragons to be different, but I guess I just was. I drop to my knees and reach out, hesitating at the last second and glancing up at his face.

He's watching me intently, his expression different from anything I've seen on him so far. The combination of that and his true features clear to see, no glamor, makes my dick ache with need. I can't look away from him, but I can feel the fabric of my new underwear becoming damp with precum.

"If you're waiting for permission to touch me, consider it granted. With no limits. Touch me anytime, anyplace." Fabian grabs my hand and wraps it around his cock.

My fingers tighten reflexively, and he groans. "Yessss, Rhys."

It's the first time he's said my name without adding "Dr." to the front, and a shiver racks me. Who knew my name could have such an effect on me?

I loosen my grip and lean in to study him more closely. His dick is… rippled? Maybe "ridged" is a better word. The bumps go all the way around and are regular distances from each other, spaced over the entire length of him… which is considerable. My hole twitches pleasurably as I imagine taking him, feeling each of those ridges breach me again and again as he thrusts.

Scrambling to my feet, I blurt, "We need the lube now."

He stares at me like I'm crazy, then steps forward to press against me and kiss me. The feel of his naked body rubbing lightly along mine is enough for me to lose all faculties. "Where is it?" he murmurs against my lips.

"Where's what?"

"Never mind." He backs me up to the bed and pushes me down onto it. "Get those briefs off."

Briefs? I blink at him.

"Get naked, Rhys, so I can fuck you until you scream."

Oh!

I've never moved so fast in my life, shoving the underwear down my legs and then hurling it away. Who knows where it lands. When I look back up at Fabian, he's smiling at me, his hand cupped and a small puddle of liquid in the palm.

"What's that?"

"Lube."

I glance around, my brain function slowly coming back online now that we're not touching. "Where'd it come from?" I'm pretty sure the bottle I brought is in the bathroom.

He shrugs. "Magic."

Huh. It'd be nice if sorcery worked that way.

He climbs onto the bed, and for the first time, nerves cluster in my belly. Is this a mistake? Is it too unprofessional? Shouldn't I be on my best behavior this weekend?

"What's wrong?" he asks.

Some of the nerves disappear. How can it be a mistake to be with someone who's so aware of my feelings?

I shrug and clear my throat. "Nothing. I just… It's been a while for me. And this whole situation is unusual."

Fabian nods. "We can stop if you want."

I hesitate. "Maybe we could slow down? I don't want to stop."

He leans over and kisses me. "What if I suck your cock while I prep you?"

I'm not sure how that would be slowing down, but I definitely don't want to say no.

"Yeah, uh… sounds good. I mean… yes. I want that." A few more nerves drift away.

"Lie back. Relax. Let me take care of you."

Those are magic words. I let him draw me down to lie against the pillows, relaxing into them. He kisses my mouth, then the side of my neck. The hollow of my throat. Both my nipples; first the left, with a tongue flick added in, then the right. The line down the center of my abdomen… though he gets distracted by my six-pack, stopping to lick each and every bump and ripple of muscle. I like working out and consider it its own reward, but even if I didn't, this would make it all worth it.

He inches his way lower and lower, his lips a slow torment against my skin until I'm writhing, desperate for him to put his mouth on my cock.

But he doesn't. Instead, he licks along the crease of my thigh, letting my leaking dick caress his cheek in what can only be called *torture*, then bends my knees up and pulls my legs wide. The cheeky grin he sends my way is my only warning before he lowers his face and goes to town rimming me.

I'm begging in a low, broken voice before he raises his head again.

"You're so good," he croons. "So perfect. You've been so patient. I'm going to suck you now, I promise."

I barely have the mental acuity to process the words, but it's okay, because he follows through, his hot, wet mouth closing around the head of my cock seconds later. The sound that leaves my throat is more sob than moan.

As his talented, wicked tongue works its magic, his fingers trace over my balls, back along my perineum, and ghost over my sensitive hole.

"Fabian," I gasp. He moans around my dick, the vibration making my eyes roll back.

And then he slides a finger inside.

The two-pronged assault on my senses is almost more than I can stand. I'm not sure if Fabian can tell or if my wordless gibbering gives it away, but it's not too long before he eases away, leaving me gasping.

"You're amazing," he tells me, admiration in his voice and gaze. "So responsive."

"It's all you," I manage. It's true—I've never been this relaxed and turned on with a virtual stranger before. Usually it takes months into a relationship. "Sorry you're doing all the work."

He chuckles, moving over me and kissing my mouth. I can taste myself on him, and the reminder of what he's done to me makes me harder than ever. "This isn't work, Rhys. It's pure pleasure."

"I still want to touch you," I insist.

"After," he promises. "We have all night."

I shiver. A whole night of this? Plus the chance to explore Fabian at my leisure?

Yessssss.

He adjusts his position between my legs, the blunt head of his cock pressing against me, and I'm suddenly struck by how intimate this is, face-to-face, limbs entangled. This is how lovers have sex, not casual hookups.

But I can't bring myself to change position.

"All good?" Fabian asks, his gaze searching mine.

"Yes. I want you in me. Don't make me wait."

He pushes forward slowly. I was right before—each ridged inch of his dick feels amazing. My muscles close around every dip, then are forced open again by the next bump. By the time he's all the way in, I'm panting.

And then he starts to withdraw, picking up the pace a little.

The second thrust has me breaking out in a sweat all over my body.

By the third, I'm keening his name. He braces himself on one arm and slides his free hand between us to close around my cock.

The fourth thrust sends me over the edge.

"Rhys!" he cries, slamming into me one more time, his head thrown back. I can't speak, all my muscles locked in the delicious agony of my orgasm.

And then finally I can breathe again, sinking into the mattress as Fabian slumps against me.

CHAPTER SEVEN

Fabian

I WAKE up feeling bone-meltingly relaxed and refreshed. Good sex always does this to me. With my eyes still closed, I slide my arm across the mattress in search of Dr. Rhys and find… nothing.

He's gone.

I lift my head and open my eyes, but he really is gone. The door to his attached bathroom is open, so I can see he's not in there. Squinting at the window, I note that while it's definitely morning, it's still early, so he could have stayed in bed for a cuddle… or another fuck.

Still, I can't be mad with him. Not after last night. Who would have guessed that my straitlaced scientist would be so creative in bed?

For a long, daydreamy moment, I stare up at the ceiling and remember allllll the things we did. Dr. Rhys should win an award. That whole shy thing is a real turn-on too. I wonder if I can convince him to let me watch him work out… naked. Or in his new underwear that somehow managed to hide nothing and everything at the same time.

Sighing, I toss back the sheet and get out of bed. Since Dr. Rhys isn't here, there's no point lazing around. Today's going to be busy, and I'd like to follow up on my thoughts about Achatius's research while I've got the chance.

Deep in thought, I stroll down the hallway and up the stairs toward my rooms on the third floor. I'm certain Achatius wrote a paper on human magic. If nothing else, I can pass a copy of that along to CSG. Their human members are having to rediscover how to use magic all by themselves, and it can't be easy.

"Fabian, what are you doing?"

Blinking, I look around and see Wil smirking at me.

"I'm going to my room."

He raises a brow. "Naked?"

"I'm not—" Wait. Did I put my clothes on before I left Dr. Rhys's room?

I look down. No. No, I did not.

"Of course naked," I declare with as much dignity as I can muster. "How else am I supposed to feel the air on my… nether region?"

His smirk turns into a grin. "Your what?"

"My nether region. It's the parts of me normally covered by underpants."

"Oh, I know that." He nods. "I just wanted you to say it again. Why didn't you just say dick?"

"Because the nether region isn't just the dick, thank you very much. There's also the balls, the perineum, and the anus. It's faster to just say nether region."

"Thank you for educating me. You know I don't believe a word you're saying, right?"

Now I frown. "Why not? It really is more than just cock. Look, I'll show you." I reach down and lift my cock out of the way, spreading my legs so my balls will be clearly visible. I'll have to turn around and bend over so he can see the rest.

"Whoa!" He holds up both hands, palms out. "That's not what I meant. You're very pretty down there, Fabian, but I don't need a show-and-tell."

"Do I even want to know?" a new voice asks exasperatedly, and we turn to see Brandt standing a few yards down the hall, Percy beside him looking resigned.

"You really don't," Wil says, cheeks bright red.

"Know what? Why not?" I look between them, confused. "I was just showing Wil what the nether region is."

"Doesn't he know? Wil, I didn't realize you were so sheltered." Brandt sounds like he's going to choke on something.

"It was fun while it lasted, but that's my cue to leave," Will announces, heading toward the stairs. "Fabian, put clothes on before you come downstairs."

"Why *are* you naked, Fabian?" Percy's voice is curious and not at all mocking, but I know Wil can still hear us, so I have no choice about what answer to give.

"I'm airing out my nether region."

Percy only hesitates for the briefest moment before saying, "Didn't Rhys give it a good airing last night?"

Brandt starts to laugh.

"He did." I nod firmly. "But a man can never be too aired out."

"There's really no response to that," Percy tells Brandt. "Try to remember your clothes in future, please," he adds pointedly to me.

I just smile.

"Let's go." Brandt puts an arm around Percy's shoulders. "Breakfast will be nearly ready, and there's no need for us to stand here examining Fabian's nether region."

"See you later!" I say, continuing toward my room. I hear their footsteps retreating behind me.

In my rooms, I walk right past my closet and into the adjoining room that serves as my office. Brandt offered me one of the parlors on the main floor, but I prefer having a cozy little space here, where fewer people are likely to walk past or walk in. Preserving the knowledge of dragonkind is hard work and needs concentration.

Fortunately, I'm a very committed person.

I settle at my desk and pick up the glass paperweight I've been using for a focus. Most dragons say glass is too fragile to conduct magic properly, but that's just because they're impatient and clumsy. A glass focus is like a cock that's just come. Eventually, you can get it up again with proper handling, but you have to be careful to avoid chafing.

Or something. It's not a perfect analogy.

It doesn't take me long to find what I'm looking for in the archive. Achatius did in fact do some detailed research into human magic, and I make a note to see if one of the elves has already had it translated and given it to CSG. Then I start reading his research on atmospheric magic here on Earth.

"Fabian?"

Blinking, I turn my head to glance up at Dr. Rhys and smile. "Hi."

His return smile is wry. "Hi, yourself. Kethe asked me to come up and see if you wanted breakfast."

I stretch slightly. "Sure, I'll come down in a bit."

He bites his lip, and I get the feeling he's trying to keep from laughing. "I don't think she'll feed you anything if you don't come down now. It's nearly ten, and she wants to start preparing for this afternoon."

"Nearly ten?" I look over at the window, and sure enough, the quality and angle of light has changed. "I could have sworn I was only working for a few minutes." I'm suddenly aware of how hungry I am. "Guess I'd better grab some food while I can." Standing, I start toward the door.

"Uh, Fabian?" Dr. Rhys's voice is strangled. "Maybe put on some clothes? As much as I enjoy the view, I don't think Kethe's the type to like nudity in the kitchen."

Sighing, I turn toward the closet. "I'd regret it for a long time." Still, I put a bit of extra sway into my step. Enjoys the view, does he?

Behind me, I hear a muffled groan, and I grin.

It only takes a moment to get dressed, but I spend a little longer choosing my rings for the day. My hoard is pitifully small compared to what it used to be. I had to leave the bulk of it behind when we fled our dying world, and five years isn't enough time to rebuild. There are fewer than a thousand pieces in the cabinet I had specially built, but they're all special and they're all mine. Dr. Rhys gasps when I open it, and I can't help feeling smug that he recognizes the glory of my hoard.

When we leave my rooms and head for the stairs, I say, "You were gone when I woke up this morning."

He side-eyes me. "Yeah. I can't stay in bed once I've woken up, and I didn't want to disturb you. You looked so peaceful."

"I wasn't peaceful," I correct. "I was satisfied. Sated. Fucked out."

His cheeks go pink. "Whatever it was, I didn't want to wake you. So I went downstairs for breakfast."

Just because I want to see if he can blush more, I say suggestively, "I could have given you breakfast."

The pink deepens, but he laughs. "I bet you could. But I was in the mood for Kethe's amazing pancakes."

"Ooh, she makes the best pancakes." I discard thoughts of teasing Dr. Rhys and pick up the pace a little. There'll be plenty of time for that later… right now, pancakes await.

Kethe grumbles about me not keeping track of time, but she feeds me nonetheless, and Dr. Rhys joins me at the table, nursing a cup of coffee and chatting to her while I eat. He has a lot of questions about dragons, and I let Kethe answer them, mentally noting to get some of the histories that have been transcribed for him to read. He'll need a translator, of course, so we can read them together. Maybe we can make it a sex game somehow. A blowjob for every chapter we read?

I'm daydreaming about how much fun that would be when Kethe whisks my plate away. I hadn't even realized it was empty.

"Come on," I tell Dr. Rhys, "I'll give you a tour of the grounds."

He blushes, and it takes me a second to realize why.

"No, I mean an actual tour. I thought maybe you'd like to see me shift."

His gasp and wide eyes are very flattering. "Yes! That would be… Is it allowed?"

I shrug. "Here at the estate, sure. Probably the only reason you haven't already seen a shifted dragon is because we have to hide from the humans."

Dr. Rhys follows me outside, and I lead the way

down to the grassy expanse we use for launching and landing. I'd planned to give him an actual tour of the grounds, but he's so excited to see me shift that it seems mean to make him wait. He's asking questions about how the shift works and what I feel when I do it, and I feel the strangest rush of affection.

Huh. Could I actually *like* Dr. Rhys? I mean, of course I like him. He's a likable person. But could I feel more for him than just friendship and sexual attraction?

Nah. He's just really cute when he gets all science-y and excited.

"Wait here," I order, stopping him well clear of the space I'll need. One thing that's been drilled into me since I was a fledgling is to *always* make sure to have plenty of room before shifting. Nobody wants to accidentally crush a friend. "Don't come closer until I've shifted, okay?"

He nods emphatically. "Okay. Um… when you've shifted, can I touch you?"

"Sure. You can climb on me too. Another day, when we have time, I'll take you flying."

His eyes almost pop out of his head. "Flying? Really? Oh, wow."

"Stay here," I remind him, then continue across the clearing until I've left twice as much room as I actually need between us.

Then I reach out to my magic.

The euphoria of the shift washes over me, tingling through every cell of my being. As much as I love my biped form, there's something about my natural dragon shape that calls to me. Nothing feels quite so comfortable. There was a time, before I accepted my current job, when I would spend weeks or even months at a time in dragon form. Sometimes I think I'd like to do that again, maybe even take longer. A few years in a remote, mountainous region, where I could play in the up and down drafts and spend my time glorying in nature and thinking.

But I won't. Aside from my responsibilities as record keeper, the plain fact is that I'd probably get bored quickly. I like being biped. Taste buds are amazing things, and sex. I can't have sex in my dragon form. It's a deficiency.

Speaking of sex and people I want to have it with… I turn my head toward Dr. Rhys, who's staring at me with his mouth open and very flattering awe on his face. I preen. I've never been one for false modesty—I know I'm very good-looking in both my forms—but there's something nice about seeing Dr. Rhys admire me.

He approaches slowly, hand held out. "Fabian?"

I nod, then wait for him to get closer and stretch my neck out to nudge his hand with my nose.

"Whoa," he breathes, grinning. "You're amazing."

I preen again. It's good that he recognizes how amazing I am. Delicately—I'm a *lot* bigger than him right now—I nuzzle his cheek. My head is about three times the size of his whole body, but I'm fully in control and have excellent coordination.

Dr. Rhys closes his eyes at the touch, then opens them quickly, as though not to miss anything. "So soft," he whispers. "I thought you'd be more scaly."

I chuff, and not just because I *am* scaly. It's just that our scales feel different from what Earth species are used to. But also, that's exactly what every single Earth person I've seen touch a dragon has said.

He puts his hand on my face and strokes, and I let

my eyes fall closed. It's nice to be petted. I wonder if I can convince him to pet me in biped form too.

"I love your coloring," he murmurs. "Kethe said dragons change color as they get older. Does that mean you're not always going to be this gorgeous pink? It's like the heart of a rose, deep and luscious."

The shiver that racks my whole body takes me by surprise. If I was in my biped body, I'd say the combination of his hand on my skin, the tone of his voice, and his words had aroused me, but in this form, I don't feel sexual desire.

Whatever it is, Dr. Rhys jerks his hand back. "Did I hurt you?" he asks anxiously. I shift closer in response, so his whole body is pressed against me, and he chuckles. "Okay, maybe not. Are you this soft all over?" He moves away from my face and lays his hands on my flank. "Oh, it feels different here. Still softer than I thought."

I stand still as he walks down the length of me, petting and stroking and mumbling to himself about scales and muscle tone and wingspan. Without him having to ask, I obligingly spread my wings, holding them aloft, and he launches into another series of muttered observations about bone structure and webbing. Maybe I should have brought someone else with us, so they could answer his questions while he admired me—because, despite his scientific focus, he's still definitely admiring—but I'm glad we're alone. I like having his attention solely on me. And I can fill in the gaps in his knowledge later. After all, if I'm going to teach a class on dragons, this will be good practice.

Finally, he gets back to my head and leans against me. "Thank you for this. You're so beautiful." He hesitates. "Would you mind walking around a bit so I can see how you move?"

Despite what a lot of Earth folklore says, we're not awkward on the ground, so I'm happy to show off for him… but not while he's standing so close. I don't want to risk that he'll accidentally get knocked over. So I nudge him gently in the direction of the house until he gets the hint.

"Oh… do you want to shift back? Okay." He sounds disappointed. "I'll wait over there."

As soon as he's at a safe distance and has turned back to look at me, I walk in a big circle. Truthfully, I feel a bit foolish doing that, but the way his face lights up soothes the pain. I'm so going to get laid later. The part of my brain that remembers sex in biped form is really excited about that, even if the rest of me doesn't care.

I do a second lap at a trot, then check to make sure he's still standing safely away and launch into the air.

His delighted cry rings in my ears as I soar upward, wings lifting me higher and higher. I meant what I said earlier—if he wants to, one day I'll take him up. I think he'd love it.

Circling the estate, I stay fairly low so he can see me clearly but sneak in some minor aerobatics. Nothing fancy—a loop and some zigzags. Enough so he can get a sense of how maneuverable I am. Finally, though, I head in to land. Our guests will start arriving soon, and I want Dr. Rhys well away from this area before then. Dragons who don't know how new he is to us might not take as much care as I am.

Dr. Rhys barely waits for me to shift back before he's running over to me. He grabs me in a huge, squeezing hug, then smacks a kiss on my mouth. "That was incredible! Thank you so much for sharing it with me."

I hold on a moment longer when he starts to pull back. Yep, my biped self really likes being pressed against him. "It was my pleasure," I say when I eventually let him go. "I bet you'd like some answers to your questions, though."

"If it's not too much trouble. But I want to make notes first." He pats his pockets, as though looking for a notepad or pen, and I take a moment to admire him. He's wearing jeans again today, dark blue ones that hug every inch of his long legs, and another short-sleeved polo shirt. It's a good look on him, very neutral and not trendy, but still attractive.

"We'll get some tea and cookies from Kethe, and you can make all the notes you want," I promise, turning in the direction of the house.

"Do you have a heightened metabolism like Earth shifters?" he asks, following me.

"Yes and no. We don't eat as much as they do all the time, but after shifting or using large amounts of magic, we need to eat more."

"That's fascinating. Kethe said you're not shifters in the same sense they are, but she didn't explain…"

I link my arm in his, welcoming the opportunity to feel him up a bit. He really does have nice musculature. "We're not. Earth shifters—felids and hellhounds—were created to be beings that can take two forms. We dragons were originally not corporeal at all. We're created from pure energy—the closest comparison is electrical impulses. A long-ago ancestor was fascinated by corporeal beings and decided to try it. They shifted from formless energy into a body they liked the idea of.

It took some time and experimentation by several of us before they decided our dragon shape was the best." He's slowed down, and I tug him to keep up.

"So… they just decided to manipulate the energy that made up their ethereal beings into physical ones?" There's awe in his voice. "Can you still do that? Become ethereal, I mean."

I shrug. "Sure. But we don't bother with it much. It's hard, and there's really not much to do except exist and think… and even then, your thoughts aren't the same without the context of touch and sight and smell and sound. A corporeal body is so much more pleasurable."

"I suppose." He sounds uncertain. "Does that mean you can change shape into any being you want?"

I side-eye him as we cross the terrace. "Technically, yes. But learning a new shape takes a lot of effort and energy, and most dragons quickly lose interest. Our natural shape and this biped one really are the best. We've evolved them over the millennia to suit our needs perfectly."

He's silent for a moment as we enter the house, then he says, "When this study is done, I'm going to spend a few centuries studying dragons. I think it will take that long."

I grin and pat his arm. "At least that long. I'd be happy to help. You can help me too—Brandt and Percy have given me the go-ahead to teach a class about dragons. Obviously it won't have so much detail as to take a few hundred years, but you can help me determine what people want to know."

"That sounds like fun." He perks up. I send him to get what he needs to take notes with, then sidle into the kitchen. Kethe is hard at work preparing for our guests, but I know better than to try to help. If she needs help, she'll put me to work. If I try to step in of my own accord, I'll get scolded, my knuckles rapped, and probably miss dessert for a week. Nobody crosses Kethe.

She glances at me. "Finished showing off?"

I sniff as I get out the mugs and a teapot. Percy showed me the proper way to make tea. "You can't call that showing off. Fledglings can fly like that."

Kethe grins. "True. But he seemed impressed anyway. He's a nice man."

"He is," I agree. "And very intelligent. He's going to consult with me on my dragon classes."

"That's unusual for you."

I stop spooning loose tea into the pot and frown at her. "What do you mean?"

She shrugs. "Just that normally you don't choose your sex partners for their personalities or intelligence. You pick someone pretty, get off, and don't see them again."

My frown deepens. She makes me sound shallow. "That's not true. I have sex with lots of nice people who I see all the time. What about Dustin?" Granted, it's been a very long time since we had sex, but it still counts.

"I'm not saying it never happens," she counters. "But you and Dustin were good friends before you had sex, if I recall correctly. And I'm not suggesting that you're callous or uncaring toward your sexual partners. I know there are many that you've run into afterward, and you're always very friendly. But have you ever met someone, recognized how nice and smart they are, had sex with them, and then wanted to continue spending time with them outside of sex?"

I open my mouth to indignantly declare that of course I have… except I haven't. I think. Kethe's right; while I have often had sex with friends or friendly acquaintances in the past, I've never met a stranger, fucked them, and then wanted to keep them around. If we weren't friends first, we never became friends after.

"What have I done?" I murmur, and Kethe's look this time is wry.

"Here we go."

"How many opportunities have I squandered?"

"Opportunities for what, Fabian?"

I fling my arms wide to encompass everything, accidentally tossing tea leaves halfway across the kitchen. "All of it! How many friendships did I miss because I was so focused on carnal pleasure? What if those people had things to teach me? I'm supposed to be learning, gathering knowledge, preserving it… how can I do that if I shut people out? I've failed in my calling."

"No, but you will if I have to kill you for messing up the kitchen. Clean up that tea, please."

I blink. Kethe's tone is calm, but that slight edge tells me she means what she says.

"Sorry," I mumble, putting down the canister and hurrying to sweep up the mess. I can't believe I've been so foolish. All those people I've waved off without a second thought. What if one of them—

"As to the rest," Kethe announces, breaking into my thoughts, "I don't think you need to be too concerned about many of your playmates being important sources of historic information. Especially not the ones you met through those apps. It's possible that you may have been able to forge friendships with some of them, given time and effort, but really, I was just commenting that it's nice to see you changing your routine. You're not meant to be alone forever."

I freeze, still crouching over the scattered tea. "What?"

She laughs. "Don't get all panicked. I'm not suggesting you need to settle down. But the fact that you're planning to spend time out of bed with Rhys means that you're beginning to appreciate that your sexual needs and your intellectual and emotional needs can be met by the same person."

Sweeping up the last of the mess, I mutter, "I don't have emotional needs." Do I? I've always been a very level-headed and emotionally stable person. Not like Dustin, who has a flair for drama and is very needy, or Steffen, who… well, we know Steffen has some emotional issues. But I'm very self-sufficient, emotionally. I have my friends and my work, and there are lots of people for me to have sex with. It all functions well. I don't need to have one special person who knows me completely. That would just be a distraction from my work.

"Everyone has emotional needs, Fabian," Kethe says patiently. "Clearly you're not as ready as I thought. I'm sorry I brought it up." She goes back to chopping vegetables, and I race through the rest of the tea preparation, lost in thought.

Could she be right? Am I actually ready for one of those relationship things?

CHAPTER EIGHT

Rhys

JUST A FEW WEEKS after Fabian came back into my life, things are so different, I hardly recognize myself. My study has blown up already—I have people clamoring to sign up, loving the idea of being able to contribute to science by having sex. All it took was some money to get the word out. Which is great, right? But the thing is, as much as all we scientists like to think we're in this for knowledge, there's a fair bit of politics involved in our work, and the second word got out that I had multi-government support, the vultures swooped. Suddenly, everyone at KRD wants to be my friend. After all, who knows how much of an "in" I have with influential people.

Sura gleefully made the whole thing much worse by "casually" mentioning my weekend at Here Be Dragons. According to the vague hints she's been dropping, Brandt and Percy consider me their new best friend. Some days it's hard to remember why we're friends.

Anyone who might have had doubts about her story lost them when Fabian came to visit a few days after that first weekend. He loudly announced to Taryn at reception that he was just stopping by for a quick visit and didn't need an appointment because we're lovers. It took about 0.75 seconds for that news to circulate through the building, another two seconds for someone to decide that must mean Brandt and Percy *actually* consider me their long-lost nephew, and less than a minute after that for me to wish I was dead.

Then Fabian wandered into the lab and kissed me, and all my troubles fell away.

That's kind of the story of these past few weeks. I'm swamped by work, slightly stressed by the idea that community species are losing their abilities, more stressed that people are hoping my research can help them… and then I'll see Fabian and kiss him and none of it seems quite so bad. I was definitely right to be worried about getting feelings for him.

On the plus side, I haven't been fucked and chucked. Fabian seems genuinely fond of me, and he definitely likes having sex with me. In fact, he's switched up his usual routine to spend most nights here in the city with me instead of going to Here Be Dragons after his classes. I'm not sure whether we're dating or just hanging out and having sex, but I like it. I like him. A lot. So maybe my heart will get a bit bruised later on, but for now, my upside-down life is great.

"What do you think?" I ask Sura anxiously. She's been reading the outline of my plan to move some of my early participants—including Fabian—to the next stage of the study, which is where I put them on a sex schedule, so to speak, to see if it's possible to control and manipulate the effect of sex on their metaphysical health.

"Looks good." She hands me back my tablet. "I don't see why you want to rush things, though. You were happy to hold off for a while longer before."

I can't tell her that the future of our species might depend on what I'm doing and that any results that might point us in the right direction would be welcome, so instead I smile vaguely and say, "I guess I want to move forward now that I can. The extra participants have got me excited."

"Got you excited, hey?" She smiles slyly. "Is it the new participants doing that, or one particular original participant?"

Heat flushes through my whole body, but I can't hold back my smile. "Stop. I'm being professional."

Her laugh makes one of the other researchers we share the lab with look up for a second. "Suuuuure, professional. You forget that I've met Fabian. 'Professional' isn't a word that applies to him."

"He's very good at his job," I defend. He really is, though. Sure, he's scattered and vague and zones out in the middle of some conversations and gets sidetracked in others, but he's completely dedicated to knowledge and its preservation. And he knows so much. His brain retains all kinds of weird facts and bits of information, and if he doesn't remember it off the top of his head, he usually knows where to look for it. He's also ridiculously easygoing and good-natured, likes to cuddle, and worships my body.

Sura just grins at me knowingly and goes back to work.

Pushing (most) thoughts of Fabian aside, I spend the afternoon contacting participants and discussing the next phase of the study with them. Most are happy to hear things are progressing and keen to be part of it. One woman jokes about finally having a decent excuse to schedule sex. I've been so lucky with my participants so far, and I hope these new ones are just as amazing.

I'm still on the phone when the lab door opens and Fabian comes in, talking over his shoulder to someone in the hall. "…disappointed. Thanks for telling me!"

I tune him out and focus on my call. "…Friday won't work, but I guess Saturday would be okay? Does it need to be at a particular time?"

"Not necessarily, but in the initial stages I'd like the timing to be consistent," I reply, my whole body itching with the urge to turn and see what Fabian is doing. I can hear the low murmur of him talking to Sura but can't make out the words. "So if it was early afternoon one week, it would be best to keep it that way for the next week too."

"Hmm," my participant says. "That might make it harder. The kids' sports are at different times every week, so I can't guarantee that."

"Let's take Saturday off the list, then," I suggest. "That leaves us with Sunday, Tuesday, and Wednesday for sure, with a question mark for Thursday. Talk to your partner and see how you both feel about those days and how many of them you can commit to. Remember that masturbation is fine, so if your partner isn't up for it, there's no pressure." I wish I didn't have to say stuff like that, but sadly, it turned out to be necessary. "And of course it's fine if you're not up for it either. Having a schedule is going to change how you feel about sex, but the whole point of this study is to make you feel better overall, so don't make yourself do something you don't want to."

He laughs. "You're sweet, but my partner and I *love* this study. It's revitalized our sex life. This is going to be fun—I can already imagine them planning something special for sex nights. I'll email you later tonight or tomorrow morning with the days that work best for us."

Thrilled by the thought of couples using my research as an excuse to jazz up their sex lives, I thank him and end the call.

"Sooooo," Fabian says, appearing beside me so suddenly, I drop the cordless handset. "You're scheduling people's sex now?" He leans in and kisses my cheek, then rests his head against mine while he peers down at my laptop screen. It's open to the master timetable, which uses participant ID numbers rather than names or any other personal details, so I let him look and luxuriate in the affectionate gesture.

"I'm scheduling people's sex," I agree. "Including yours, if you're okay with that."

He straightens and turns his wide-eyed gaze on me. "Really?"

"Only if you don't mind." I'm not quite sure how to read that response.

"That could be amazing fun! Wait... it's not just once a week, is it?"

I hide a smile at the note of alarm in his voice. "No, it can be as often as you think you'll want, but it needs to be planned out beforehand. And then in a few months, we'll change it up and see what impact that has."

Fabian purses his lips. "So I could schedule for every night of the week?"

My stomach cramps slightly, because I don't see him every night of the week. Does this mean he's having sex with other people? We never talked about being exclusive, so that's his right, but I definitely don't want to hear about it. I haven't had to check the data at individual level since we started sleeping together, and now I'm suddenly afraid of what I'll find when I do.

But I paste on an expression of professional detachment and say, "Theoretically, yes, but if you were going to do that, I'd want it to be at the same time down to the minute, and then when we change the schedule, either frequency or timing would need to change dramatically."

He wrinkles his nose and shakes his head. "That doesn't sound sexy at all. But I don't have sex every night anyway. This just means it'll be official." He sounds somewhat doubtful, and I figure it's that old "I don't *need* to, but I like to know I can" situation.

"If you're sure you're okay with it?" I check, and he nods determinedly.

"Yes. Okay, so it has to be in the evenings, because you work during the day. And I can't come to the city on Wednesdays because my classes run late, so not Wednesday."

It's a good sign that he's factoring in my schedule too, right? I dutifully take down notes.

"And you have your weekly meeting thing on Monday afternoons, and you're cranky after that," he adds, "so probably not Mondays."

Oh my... I can't believe he said that.

I mean, it's true. The weekly update meeting on Monday always puts me in a bad mood, but I didn't think it was bad enough for him to notice after only three Mondays. And I especially didn't think it was bad enough for him to think I wouldn't want sex after.

Which is partly true—I generally don't feel sexy on a Monday, but with a little effort that can change.

Worst of all, though, is that he said it *here*, with Sura and one of my other colleagues within earshot.

Kill. Me. Now.

"Uh," I mutter, not sure what to say.

Fabian doesn't seem to notice. "I like to be at home on the weekend, since Brandt and Percy come back then. Would you be okay with coming to stay at Here Be Dragons on the weekends? We don't have to always go on a Friday night—Saturday morning would be okay."

Okay, this is starting to sound really couple-y, and I can't deny how good that feels. "That's fine," I manage, mentally abandoning all the work I usually do on the weekends. I'll have an assistant as soon as I get around to hiring them, and then they can pick up some of the slack. Plus, Fabian might not be a workaholic in the same league as me, but he does usually put in some time on the weekends. Mostly because he loves it so much.

"So that's Tuesday, Thursday, Friday, Saturday, and Sunday," he sums up. "That sounds reasonable."

"Uh-huh." I worry my lower lip between my teeth. Does he mean to have sex with me on all those days, or am I going to be weekends only? I guess I'll find out.

"Great! And that means we can still do what we planned tonight." He leers at me, and my face gets hot, because yep, my colleagues heard that too. And Sura will have no qualms about—

"What did you have planned for tonight?"

—asking. I sigh and turn my chair to look at her. "None of your business." It's not kinky enough to interest her, anyway. Role play isn't something she's into, unless it's super weird. I know because she has no boundaries.

She gives me a look that says she'll ask again, but Fabian's already lost interest in talking about it and is ready to get started on doing it. His hand, which was innocently on my shoulder while he leaned in to read my notes, is sliding slowly down my back. Way down. Allll the way down. Until… yep, there it is, on my ass.

"Fabian," I hiss, shifting on the stool in an attempt to dislodge him. He sighs and drops his hand.

"Workplace boundary?"

I nod. "Workplace boundary." That's something I had to implement the second time he came in and wanted to give me a blowjob at my desk in the *shared* office. I've heard the rumors in the break room and know that some people have been caught doing worse, but I'm not the kind of person who can casually get it on in a semi-public place. The stress would kill me.

"Are you nearly ready to go, then? Is there anything I can help with?" He looks around—for what, I have no idea. I give in to the inevitable and begin shutting down the computer. It's not like I want to stay here and work when I could go home with Fabian, anyway.

"Two minutes," I promise.

LATER THAT NIGHT, lying naked and sweaty on my bed, still tangled up with my dragon lover, I can't imagine why I'd ever want to work when I could be doing this. Fabian's slowly running his hands through my hair, petting me, and my body is heavy and sated, muscles relaxing in a way they never have before. There's something about him that lets me be so completely at ease, even in this moment, when I'm so vulnerable.

"If there was one thing you could do, what would it be?" he asks suddenly in a low voice.

I drag my brain back from the edge of slumber and think about it. "Just one thing? Any one thing, no limits?"

"Anything, no limits. No, wait. One limit. It has to be something just for you. Something selfish. Not ending world hunger or anything like that."

Okay, that helps narrow things down a lot. "I'd read. Just read everything I could get my hands on. There's so much research out there, but I usually only have time to read the papers pertinent to my field. Sometimes I squeeze in something just for fun, but if I could do any one thing, no limits, I'd read every research study in every field that I could."

He stops petting my hair. "That sounds like fun. It almost makes me want to change mine."

"What's yours?" I don't move my head from where it's resting on his shoulder, hoping he'll start stroking me again.

"I'd walk through the meadow that used to be near my home when I was a child. The way it was then, of course. And I'd sit there and just take it all in until it was burned into my brain so I could never forget."

My heartbeat pounds in my ears as I lie still in his arms. I feel like he's given me a gift—a piece of himself. Because while I can, conceivably, read a lot of research papers in my life, maybe even retire and spend all my time doing that, he can never go back to his home. He can never revisit his childhood haunts. None of the dragons or elves I've met talk about it much, but from what I've heard, the loss of their homeland was a long, painful, traumatic process, filled with destruction and death. And now it's gone forever, the dimension collapsed in on itself and reduced to nothingness.

All they have left are memories.

Quietly, I ask, "What was it like? You don't have to tell me," I add quickly. I don't want to cause him unnecessary pain.

"No, I want to." He pauses, sighs. "I used to think my memories were clouded by how young I was, or by the contrast with what came after. But when I got this job and gained access to the living archive, I realized it wasn't true. If anything, my memories don't do it justice. It really was that beautiful." He pauses again. "Different from here. Earth is beautiful too, but it's like comparing a flower and a starry night. Each is spectacular in its own way."

I stay silent, snuggling just a tiny bit closer.

"The grass in my meadow was orange, a rich burnt shade, and when the wind blew and it rippled, the color would shift. I used to watch it for hours. And the tréghel trees... you've met David. Did you notice the necklace he wears?"

"Yes." It's hard to miss, even though he keeps it tucked into his clothes a lot of the time. The chain is unusual enough in itself, but the pendant is stunning. It's in the shape of a leaf, but one I don't recognize, a perfect gold color, and it glows. At first I just thought it was the way the light reflected off it, but no—it definitely glows.

"That's a tréghel leaf. Caolan brought it through the portal for him and preserved it with a spell. Imagine a tree full of those leaves... a forest of those trees. The warm light of the tréghel groves was a beacon on the darkest of nights. And they were always teeming with life—birds, small animals…" He sighs again. "I think I miss those trees more than anything."

The scientist in me knows why they couldn't bring a sapling or two with them, but my emotional brain hates that they had to leave it all behind. Right this second, I'd give almost anything just so Fabian could see a tréghel tree again.

"I wish…" I let it trail off. There's nothing I can say that will make this easier for him, even five years on. Probably not even five hundred years on.

He starts petting my hair again. "I know. Me too."

CHAPTER NINE

Fabian

I'VE BEEN on a sex schedule for a month now, and I'm surprised by how much I like it. Sure, it means some days I'm absolutely not allowed to have sex or even jerk off, no matter how much I want to, but it adds a very sensual element of anticipation. Knowing that *today* I'm not allowed but *tomorrow* I can builds the longing. Every second that passes is a delightful tease. Rhys is the master of edging without even saying a word.

Which is why I'm here at the lab instead of in class like I'm supposed to be. I couldn't wait until tomorrow to see him, even if we can't have sex today. I just want to hear his voice and see his beautiful eyes and that smile he saves just for me. The one that says he thinks I'm nuts but he can't help smiling anyway.

I wave to Chris and Taryn, who've long since given up asking me if I have an appointment and trying to make me wait while they call Rhys, and breeze past them to the corridor that leads to Rhys's lab. At this time of day, he should be elbow deep in analyzing data. It's one of the best times to watch him, because he gets this cute little furrow between his eyebrows and his focus is so intense, he doesn't know what's going on around him. Maybe I can just slip in and watch him for a while without him noticing. And then when he finally stops to take a break, I can be all "surprise!" And we can have some sneaky kisses.

This is an excellent plan.

I'm halfway down the hall when I see Rhys up ahead. He's talking to someone… a man. They're standing very close, heads bent together, and… are they holding hands?

As I watch, the other man removes his hand, and I can see now that Rhys is holding his phone and they're both looking at it. Still… was the touching necessary? And do they really need to stand that close?

I pick up my pace and call out, "Hi, Rhys!"

They both look up, and Rhys's face lights up with a smile, then falls as he glances sideways at the other man. What the fuck?

I do *not* like this whole situation.

Reaching them, I lean in and kiss Rhys like I always do. Maybe it's a little more intense than usual.

He pulls back.

He… pulls back?

He *pulls back*.

I blink at him in shock and disbelief.

"Fabian, this is Dr. Rafter, the director of Kendall Research and Development," he says, his cheeks pink and eyes wide, before he turns to *that man*. "Sir, I'd like you to meet Fabian Draco, the record keeper and historian for dragonkind."

The man holds out his hand to me. "It's a pleasure to meet you, Mr. Draco."

I shake his hand, mostly because I want to get his measure, but also because if he's the director here, that makes him Rhys's boss. "It's nice to meet you too."

He's a demon, which makes him too big. I bet he thinks he's special because he's all tall and big. How would he feel if I shifted into my dragon form and stepped on him? Then we'd see who the big one is.

But the benefit of him being a demon is that his shields aren't as tightly locked as Rhys's. He's clearly had a sorcerer build him a good one, but I still get very strong impressions from him. He's oddly calm and analytical for a demon, very focused and driven, and he's… amused by me? I resist the urge to give him an electric shock and put him in his place. I've got scales older than his grandparents, and *he's* amused by *me*? Pah!

He glances over at Rhys, and I instantly get the impression of admiration—which makes sense; it's Rhys—and warmth. I drop his hand. How dare he have warm feelings for my Rhys!

"You must be very busy," I say. "We wouldn't want to keep you."

Rhys makes a strangled sound, then coughs. "I can send you that information this afternoon," he offers. "And then of course I'm happy to go through it with you at your convenience."

I frown.

"If you have a moment now, I'll come to the lab with you and you can show me that trend graph. The rest can wait until Monday's meeting," Dr. Rafter says. He's not actually smiling at Rhys, but it still seems like he is. I've noticed that demons are like that sometimes.

"Of course," Rhys says. "Ah, Fabian, did you need something or will I see you later?"

"I can wait." I smile cheerfully at him. "I want to see the trend graph too." I've actually already seen it, since Rhys updates it daily, but I came to spend time with Rhys and I'm not leaving just because his demon boss is here, having warm admiring feelings. Maybe even especially not because of that.

Rhys smiles weakly and leads the way to the lab.

Sura looks up when we enter, and her eyes widen. "Sir! Uh, hi." She scrambles to her feet. "Can I get you anything?"

I glare at her. How come she's all flustered by him but not me? I am a *dragon*.

"No, thank you, Dr. Singh. I just came to see Rhys's results. Don't let me interrupt you."

Why does he call Rhys by his first name and Sura by her title? I don't like this at all.

I like it even less when he starts asking questions about the data and my Rhys lights up the way he always does when he's talking about his research. I love that he's happy, and sure, it's great that his boss recognizes how awesome he is, but can't he recognize it from a distance? And without touching. Why does he have his hand on Rhys's shoulder when he leans in to look at the screen? That's *my* trick to touch Rhys at work.

Finally he straightens. "Well, you're doing great work, Rhys. This study is going much better than I initially thought." He squeezes Rhys's shoulder, then follows that up with a few pats.

Then he *finally* lets go and turns to me. "I hope to see you again soon, Mr. Draco. Perhaps Rhys can bring you along to one of our lunches?"

"Perhaps," I say, proud of myself for not demanding to know what lunches he's talking about. Percy's voice is in my ear, reminding me that I'm a representative of all dragons and that we want people to think the best of us.

He does that almost-but-not-really demon smile, and then leaves.

I round on Rhys. "What was that about?"

He blinks at me. "Oh… I'm sorry I didn't kiss you. I thought it might be awkward in front of the director, especially here at work."

Something in me relaxes at hearing him call Dr. Rafter "the director" instead of something more familiar. "Why are you having lunches with him?"

"I'm… not?" Rhys looks bewildered.

Behind me, Sura starts to laugh. "Ooh, I think Fabian might be a little jealous."

I scoff. "Of course I'm not." Am I? I've never been jealous before, so I don't know exactly what it feels like. "Why did he say you were having lunches together?"

There's an odd expression on Rhys's face. He's frowning, but somehow also looks delighted?

"He didn't? Do you mean when he said I should bring you to one of the monthly investor lunches?"

Oh. "Why would I go to one of those?"

Sura chokes, she's laughing so hard.

Rhys shrugs. "Because you're a dragon with a lot of money, you're close to Brandt, and the director is always on the lookout for new investors?"

I snort. "He's not very good at reading people if he thinks I'm a good investor prospect." Trying not to sound smug about it, I step closer to Rhys and lean in. "Can I have a proper kiss now?"

The frown turns into a smile, and I get a proper kiss.

But once again, he pulls away too soon.

"Rhys," I whine.

"Is that why you were being weird? You were jealous? Of *the director*?" He makes it sound stupid.

"I really don't think it was jealousy. I just didn't like the way he kept touching you. And he called you 'Rhys,' but Sura 'Dr. Singh,'" I point out.

"Yeah, I noticed that too," Sura chimes in. "I just figured it was because Rhys is his current favorite, what with the huge multi-government grant and all. But maybe Fabian's right and it's because he's hot for you."

"For the love of…" Rhys closes his eyes and takes a deep breath. "He's *not* hot for me. Nothing inappropriate happened. I ran into him in the hallway, and he asked me about the study, so I showed him some of the data. That's it."

"But he touched you," I remind him. This is kind of fun now that the director's gone and I'm the one with my hands all over Rhys.

"He didn't touch me. Not like *that*. It was… I don't know. He touched you too."

Sura and I stare at him. "You mean when he shook my hand? That's not the same thing." Seeing how flustered he's getting, I ease up. "Well, I guess it's okay. He's gone, and I'll just make sure I'm not here to see it if he touches you again." Although just the thought of it makes me feel all growly and sulky.

Rhys still seems unsure, but he lets me pet him back to happy. "Don't you have class right now? It's Wednesday." He turns his head to kiss my palm.

"I do, but I thought I could watch you work for a while and then convince you to leave early. We're not scheduled to have sex tonight, but that doesn't mean we can't tease each other, right? And I could maybe blow y —" His hand over my mouth muffles the last word.

"Fabian," he hisses, looking around wildly, even though Sura's the only other one here. "I'm at work!"

It's my turn to kiss his palm, and then I peel it away from my face. "I wasn't going to blow you here," I reason. "And I'm sure Sura's familiar with the expression."

"The expression, sure," she agrees.

"See?"

Rhys just looks at me, then sighs. "Let me finish up a few things, and then I guess I can leave early. An hour?"

"Done!" I grin victoriously. "I'll just sit over here and watch you."

"Yeah, about that... you don't literally mean watch me, do you? Like... you're going to read or work yourself or something, right?"

"Sure," I agree, because he looks worried. I'll just wait until he's in his zone of focus, and then I'll watch him.

But first...

I grab his shirt and pull him to me. "Kiss," I demand. He slides a sideways glance at Sura, who laughs out loud.

"I'll just stand outside and guard the door. You have five minutes."

I don't even wait for her to leave before my mouth is on Rhys's, and this time, I get a real kiss.

<hr>

CHAPTER TEN

<hr>

Rhys

I STUDY the faces around the table and wish I'd been able to deliver better news. While I know nobody expected me to perform miracles, I'm sure they were all hoping for one.

It's not that my news was bad. In fact, it was good… maybe even excellent. In the three months since CSG and the DEA began endorsing my study, it's grown immensely, with people still signing up every day. After all, this is the kind of medical research they're happy to help with—they don't have to do anything, take anything, or donate anything. They just go about their lives. The influx of participants has already led to more data that's changed our tack somewhat. The addition of several people on the ace spectrum was a huge benefit. It's certain that regular sex or sexual relief can boost metaphysical health in people who find pleasure that way, but we're learning that other activities can have similar effects—as can foreplay. Funnily enough, it was Fabian who helped me with that discovery. His request a while back that I "tease" him on the nights he wasn't scheduled for sex led to new data that's been really helpful.

But while the effects on metaphysical health are indisputable, they're not reversing the larger deterioration. I've played around with sex schedules for those who are on them, fine-tuning things to optimize the strength of their abilities, but we haven't seen any sign of increasing or improving them. And we probably won't until and unless someone discovers what's causing the deterioration.

Which is the reason for so many tired faces at this meeting. Sure, this problem has been developing slowly over thousands of years, but the pace has seemingly picked up over the last few centuries, and we don't know if it will continue to do so. We also don't know what it will take to rectify it… because we don't know what caused it. So while my study can help, it's only a stopgap measure, and there's only so much gap it can stop up.

Imani, who's chairing the meeting today, wraps things up. "We're doing good work," she reminds us all. "Sooner or later we're going to find the information we need." We all rally a bit because she's likely right. It's out there somewhere, and we're putting a lot of resources into the search.

I have to cling to that. My sorcery *is* me. Losing it wouldn't be survivable. Knowing future generations would lose it… well, I don't want to think about that.

It's late enough in the day that I decide not to go back to the lab. My decision is only partly influenced by the fact that Fabian's driving in after his classes today and spending the night. He'll probably be at my place already—and yes, he has a key.

I'm not really sure what's going on between us.

We're friends, and we're working together in an ad-hoc kind of way. He's my go-to source for information about dragons and dragon magic, and usually about elves too. He also has access to a ton of information about community species and Earth from before the species wars, information that we all thought was lost forever. I don't think any of our archivists realize exactly how the living archive works. They seem to assume that because the dragons and elves fled their world, they weren't able to keep all their records, that any information they give us is from memory. Which is partly true, since dragons and elves are much more long-lived than us. But also, their archive is a living construct maintained by their own innate power. At birth, every elf and every dragon is linked by a spell to the living archive. It's something they can't feel, that doesn't impact them in any way, except once they die, the sum of their memories is uploaded to the archive. Access to this is limited to archivists and historians, people like Fabian whose job it is to manage and curate. So dragons and elves today have access to all the knowledge of every one of them who ever died.

When Fabian explained it to me, it took me a while to get over my shock. He then went on to explain that the archive also contains the more common scholarly works and research, transcripts of conversations, pictures—or rather images—of items that no longer exist… the usual thing you'd find in archives. But the memories are the core of it.

Aside from being friends and sort-of colleagues, we're… I don't know. We never miss a chance to have sex. I hadn't thought I'd even want to have sex this much, but I resent the time we're apart and can't. It's not just sex, though. We really are friends, and we talk and cuddle and watch TV together. I miss more than just fucking him when he goes home… I miss him. Sura, who was initially exultant about my "return from sexual exile," has started watching me worriedly. She says the line between friends who fuck and boyfriends is a fine one, and she doesn't want me to get hurt if it blurs too much. I can't even argue with that, because I'm veering dangerously close to thinking of Fabian as my boyfriend, and I don't think he's there.

Don't get me wrong, he's definitely… well, for want of a better word, he's fond of me. He likes me. He enjoys my company, both in and out of the bedroom. Despite not being science-minded himself, he understands the nature of research, of painstakingly setting something up and studying it in great detail, reviewing data over and over again and coming to a conclusion. His research works differently, of course, but the basic principle is the same. He's just as dedicated to his work as I am. The time we spend together is never awkward or uncomfortable. I'm nearly one hundred percent sure I'm the only one he's sleeping with right now. I didn't ask that of him, and I wouldn't ask that of him, not while this thing between us is so undefined, but I can't deny I like the idea. I'm not fucking anyone else either, of course. Considering what a wasteland my sex life was before, it would feel weird to go from that to multiple partners in such a short time.

So… I guess you could say my personal life is just as interesting as my professional one right now.

When I finally walk through the door from my garage into my kitchen, I find Fabian sitting on a stool at the counter, intent on his laptop, the glass paperweight he likes to hold while accessing the living archive in his hands… and wearing only his underwear.

There's probably a perfectly logical reason. It won't be sexual—if he'd stripped off in preparation for having sex, he'd have gotten completely naked and then not allowed himself to get distracted by work. Fabian's mind might work in interesting ways sometimes, but it always follows a logical pattern.

It's just that Fabian's logic can be unique.

Rather than disturb his concentration, I go to my bedroom and change into sweatpants and a T-shirt, then log in to the lab server from my laptop and quickly check my emails. When I go back to the kitchen, he's waiting for me, a smile on his face.

"You're home early! And wearing my favorite pants." The smile changes to a leer, and heat stirs in me. He's made no secret of how much he loves my body, and my old, clingy, worn sweatpants are a particular favorite of his. That might be part of the reason I wore them instead of a newer pair.

"How long have you been here?" I ask instead. He had morning classes and then a study group but wasn't sure whether he was going to go to them all.

"Since about three. I skipped the study group. They're so intense sometimes." He shrugs, and I bite back a smile.

"Unlike you, they need to get good grades so they can get good jobs." Although he's double majoring in literature and history, so I'm not sure how many of his classmates will actually be able to achieve that goal. Fabian's just there to learn more about Earth, of course. He comes out with some mind-boggling questions occasionally, especially after he's been reading fiction.

"I suppose they are human, with short lifespans. There's not a lot of time for them to get things done. What are we having for dinner?" He slides off the stool and walks toward me, and I'm reminded that he's nearly naked.

"Uh, I'm not sure. There's not a lot in the house. Fabian, why are you only wearing underwear?"

Only a few feet away, he stops and glances down. "Oh. I spilled soda on myself, and it felt sticky and gross. I thought I'd wash my clothes." He glances around, frowning.

"Did you? Wash them?" I prompt, and he shakes his head.

"No. I was going to, but then I thought of something and… I think they're in the laundry room still." He turns and strolls in that direction, and I follow, my eyes on his ass in those close-fitting briefs. Fabian might not have the same muscle definition I do, but his body is still divine, slender and toned, and just watching him has all kinds of memories rising.

I shake away my lascivious thoughts and hurry to catch up.

In the laundry room, the door to the washer is open, and I can see his T-shirt and jeans inside. On the counter above, the lid is off the detergent. Fabian swoops in and grabs the bottle. "Thanks for reminding me, or I would have had to wear sticky, crumpled clothes tomorrow," he says over his shoulder as he carefully pours detergent into the little drawer. I watch closely while trying to look like I'm not. Kethe told me she taught everyone at Here Be Dragons how to do their own laundry but that I should keep an eye on Fabian anyway because he occasionally gets distracted

and does it wrong. This wasn't exactly a surprise to me
—I, of all people, know exactly how easily Fabian can
zone out of real life. But he does it perfectly this time,
putting the detergent away and starting the machine like
an expert.

"So," he says, turning to me, "dinner? We could
order in and eat in our underwear. Or naked!"

"Naked dinner sounds good."

LATER THAT NIGHT, we lie tangled together on the couch
in the darkened living room, pretending to watch TV. I
say pretending because Fabian has yet to get through an
episode of *The Witcher* without getting horny, no matter
what's happening on screen. If I didn't already know
how attracted to me he is, I'd develop a complex about
it. As it is, I'm secure enough in myself—and the knowledge that any second now, Fabian is going to abandon
the show completely—to also enjoy perving on Henry
Cavill in a blond wig.

Fabian turns his head and licks my neck, and I smile
into the darkness, sliding my hand over his hip.

But then he surprises me. "This is nice."

I hesitate, not sure where he's going. "What is?"

"Cuddling and watching TV. I've never done this
before."

It takes me a moment to process that. We do this all
the time, so he must mean he's never done this with
anyone else… but that's so hard to believe. Fabian is a
toucher. He has no inhibitions about casual contact with
his friends. How could he have never curled up on a
couch with someone before?

"Oh." It's inane, and I regret it the second the sound leaves my mouth, but he just chuckles.

"Normally I like to actually watch. Or it's a precursor to sex. Which this is too, because I have plans for you, but also it's nice just snuggling with you."

"I like it too." I want to say more, maybe ask what's going on with us, but I don't. This is a happy moment. It's good. I don't want to ruin that by bringing questions into it.

He kisses the spot he licked before. "Kethe says you're meeting my physical *and* emotional needs. Maybe she's right."

I stay quiet, but my hold on him tightens a little.

"Do you want to go for a flight this weekend?"

I jerk upright, accidentally sending him sprawling to the floor. "Fuck, I'm sorry!" I reach over to flip on a lamp, and we both blink in the sudden brightness. "That wasn't on purpose."

He chuckles, accepting my hand to help him back up. "Of course it wasn't on purpose. I'm no good to you on the floor." He settles on the cushion beside me, drawing his legs up. "Does this mean you don't want to go flying?"

I shake my head vehemently. "It means I *absolutely* want to go!" We've been talking about this for months, but the timing never lined up.

His face lights up with his smile. "Great! I'll tell Kethe you're spending the weekend with us." He crawls into my lap. "Now, don't we have things to do?"

"We absolutely do," I assure him, pulling him closer and melding our lips together. He kisses me with his usual combination of all-in enthusiasm and delicate skill, and it's a real effort not to get lost in the maelstrom of sensations that want to overcome me. But I want this to be about Fabian. He loves taking charge in the bedroom, loves lavishing me with attention, and it's so easy to just let him take care of everything. Sometimes, though, I like to switch things up.

Like now.

I wrap my arms around him and turn my body so he's under me on the couch. He breaks the kiss with a sound of surprise and looks up at me, puffy pink lips parted. "What—?"

"Just lie back and enjoy."

His startled expression morphs to pleasure, and he relaxes into the couch.

I can't resist another kiss, and of course it gets out of control, because his lips are a dream. But I can feel his cock against mine, both of them hard and needy, and I want so badly to get him off. If only I didn't have to stop kissing him.

Or do I?

Tentatively, I rock my hips against his.

He shifts to accommodate, grinding back.

Yeah, okay, this could work. I haven't done it this way for a very long time, but some of the hottest moments of my youth involved fully dressed writhing.

Fabian chooses that moment to break our kiss and bury his face in the side of my neck, lips working along my skin in a way that sends shivers through me. My thoughts blur together as I begin a slow, steady, thrusting grind, whispering kisses into his soft hair.

His moan vibrates through my whole body, and I pick up the pace a little. "Having fun?" I murmur, and the little laugh he gives is choked off by my next thrust.

"This might be the most fun I've ever had." He lifts

his head and turns it to meet my searching lips. "Science is not the only thing you're amazing at."

This time it's my laugh that's cut off, and I give myself over to all the delicious sensations swarming through me. Fabian in my arms, his smell, his warm skin, the taste of him on my tongue, his hard dick separated from mine by a few measly layers of fabric. Our breath speeding up, sweat beading on my skin, thrust, thrust, thrust—

"Rhys!" Fabian's whole body goes taut, and mine follows a second later.

When I can think again, I become aware of the stickiness in my pants, but can't bring myself to care. I'll deal with it in a minute. For now, I'd rather just lie here with Fabian nestled against me, his face buried in my neck again.

A stray thought pops into my head. "If flying is anything like that, this is going to be the best weekend ever."

I WAKE JUST before dawn on Saturday morning with an armful of warm, sexy dragon draped over me. For a moment, I savor the feeling.

Sura's one hundred percent right. I'm going to end up hurt. Because I'm so close to losing my heart to Fabian, and I'm not sure he's ready for it.

Sighing, I carefully ease out from under him and get dressed. Wil's probably about to go for a run, and he doesn't mind my company.

Sure enough, when I get downstairs I find Wil in the kitchen, stretching. Steffen's there too. He doesn't always come with us, but when he does, I'm not sure what to make of him. He's the dragon I've spent the least amount of time with, though it doesn't take a lot of time in his company to see that he's a conspiracy theorist and mildly paranoid. Fabian said he's been better in the last few months, which makes me wonder how bad he was before. I get the feeling he doesn't like me that much, though I'm not sure if that's me personally or his general distrust of people. Regardless, we tolerate each other well enough to go on a run together.

"Fabian still asleep?" Wil asks indulgently. Aside from Fabian and Sophie, who I talk to a lot for work, Wil's the dragon I know best. He's less intense than the rest of them (though that doesn't count for a lot when talking about dragons), and he seems to think of Fabian and Dustin as his surrogate younger brothers. Or maybe cousins. People he has to look out for and tease.

"Yep. I'll bring coffee up to him later and see if I can drag him down for breakfast." It's a fifty-fifty chance. He's generally an early riser, and he loves Kethe's breakfasts, but if he's gotten stuck into work, he might not want to leave it.

"Let's go," Steffen says. "I need to be back for a call in an hour."

We leave through the mudroom that opens onto the parking area. There's a faint trail—beaten by running feet—behind it that circles the property. Since Steffen's with us and Brandt's home, we'll be staying on the estate. Neither of them will go farther from Brandt than that when there's no other member of the security team around. It makes Brandt laugh and roll his eyes, but Steffen's in charge of security, and he gets to make the rules. It doesn't bother me—three full circuits of the trail is a good run, and there are worse places to be than Here Be Dragons.

Steffen takes the lead, and Wil falls into step with me. "So you're going flying today?" he asks between measured breaths.

"That's what Fabian said. The weather looks clear." I squint up through the trees at the sky. Last time we planned to fly, a storm blew in, and Fabian insisted my first time shouldn't be in the rain.

"Yep, it's gonna be a gorgeous day," Wil agrees. "And not windy, either. Perfect for your first time. Fabian will be gentle."

I can't hold in my snort. "Are you being serious or making innuendoes?"

Wil misses a step, almost trips, recovers, and laughs. "That was totally unintentional. I just meant that he won't do anything too fancy or complicated… and yeah, that still sounds like I'm talking about sex, doesn't it?"

"Only to those of us with sex on the brain."

We run in silence for a while. There's something so soothing about it, the steady, rhythmic cadence of my steps and breathing, the air rushing over my warm skin, the rustle of trees and sound of birdsong. Even the slight strain as my body begins to tire is comforting. I know how much further I can push it, know how it will feel when I'm done. Exercise has become such an intrinsic part of my routine that I struggle to get through the day if I haven't done any. My body has become used to it.

It's not the same for the dragons I'm running with. From talking to Fabian, I know that their bodies, while technically the same as the elves, are also not like anything else in existence. They can use their magic for everything—they don't need to eat, can maintain peak fitness without exercise, don't need to physically groom themselves, don't need sex to reproduce…. Everything they do, eating, sleeping, working out, showering, sex, is because they enjoy it. In that sense, dragons are the most enthusiastic species in existence. They love experiences, love doing things, even ordinary things. I work out because I want to maintain fitness, and my brain and body have come to depend on regular exercise. Wil and Steffen work out because it's an experience they enjoy. If they decided not to do it anymore, they could still remain as fit.

It's a mindfuck.

It also gets me thinking. If you look at the spectrum of species that existed between our two planets, you have the dragons at one end, who are capable of altering almost anything about themselves. If they decide tomorrow that they want to become an aquatic species, they can evolve gills. After that come the elves and our community species here on Earth. While the elves can choose to live just as long as dragons, in every other way they're much more like us. They have a set corporeal body and abilities and live within those structures. And at the far end of the spectrum are humans, who seem to have got the dud end of the stick. They have short lives and no abilities. There isn't a single human today who has lived as long as I have, and I'm still young. My point is… what's the point? What's the purpose in having two such outlying species?

I'm still pondering that forty-five minutes later when I go back up to Fabian's room, sweaty and breathing hard. I find him sitting cross-legged in the center of his bed, still naked, his glass paperweight in hand as he stares seemingly at nothing.

Leaving him to his work, I shower and dress, and when I come out of the bathroom, he's put the paperweight away and is grabbing clothes from his closet.

"Nice run?" he asks, tilting his face toward me as I pass. I obediently kiss him, then make it two more steps before realizing what a boyfriendly thing that is to do.

"Uh, yeah." I stumble over the words. Does Fabian know we're acting like a couple? Is he doing it on purpose? "You should come one time."

He shrugs. "Maybe. Running is fine when it's taking you somewhere, but running for running's sake seems boring."

The laugh takes me by surprise. "Hurry up and get dressed. I'm starving. Oh," I add as he disappears into the bathroom, "ask me later about the spectrum of abilities across species."

He reappears in the doorway, frowning. "The what?"

I shrug. "Just something I've been thinking about that I thought you and the archive might be able to help with. It's not important… a passion project, I guess." How long has it been since I've thought about anything except my research? It can't be a bad thing for me to have something to play with on the side. Changing focus occasionally will keep me fresh.

"Okay," he agrees. "You should just go down. I'm going to be a while in the shower—Dustin found this new body scrub, and I want to try it out."

I perk up, because that means his skin will be even softer and smoother than usual tonight. "Oh yeah? Does it smell as good as that coffee one you used a few weeks back?"

He purses his lips. "Not sure. This one says it smells

like peaches. I guess it depends how much you like peaches, right?"

I don't trust myself to reply to that.

"ARE YOU READY?" Percy asks me. He's just finished checking that I'm properly strapped into the harness on Fabian's back. I take a deep breath and ignore the nervous flutters in my stomach.

"I'm ready." I reach down and pat Fabian's soft scales. They're so delightfully supple. It wouldn't be a hardship to just stroke him all day. But then, that's true no matter what form he's in. "This is going to be amazing."

Percy studies me, then simultaneously grins and shakes his head. "It will be. Have fun." He jumps down to the soft grass below, then strolls away. Fabian turns his huge head to watch, probably making sure he's clear, then glances over his shoulder at me.

I grin. This is going to be epic. It's hard to tell, but I think Fabian agrees with me.

The next moment, I feel the muscles beneath me bunch, and we're leaping up, into the air. His wings snap out, stretching wide behind me, and we climb much faster than I would have thought we could. Soon we're above the trees, above the house, waaaaaaay above, and I let out a triumphant yell. I may be a buttoned-up scientist, but I guess I still have a primal side buried deep down inside me, and this—riding on a dragon's back, *flying*—brings it out of me.

Fabian starts by flying in a big circle over the estate, giving me time to get used to his movements, to the sensation of the air flowing over me, around me. I can see so far from up here, the countryside laid out before me like a beautiful illustrated map. Fabian explained to me that he's using a distortion shield, which allows only certain people to see him. Any humans who happen to glance up right now won't notice him at all. Which is good, because reports—and phone camera footage—of a dragon flying overhead would definitely grab attention.

Fabian huffs as we complete our second circle, and I lean forward and rub his neck. "I'm ready for you to show off," I shout.

For a second, as he keeps flying placidly, I think he hasn't heard me. But then he banks sharply to the right, and I yell again. It might have been "Yee-ha!" this time. Don't judge me.

It's a good thing I have a cast-iron stomach, because Fabian puts it through its paces. We do loops. Loop-de-loops. We play keep-away with some of the taller trees. He takes me up so high, I begin to feel breathless, and then we dive, the ground zooming toward us so fast, I wonder if he can possibly pull up in time.

He does, of course. It's exhilarating.

When he tires of showing me how skilled he is at aerobatics, we go for a leisurely flight to the city. What takes hours to drive is only a twenty-minute flight, even at this steady pace. If I thought riding on dragonback was trippy out in the country, it's *wild* when we're flying over the city. Fabian even slows to do a circle over my house.

By the time we get back to Here Be Dragons and he settles us gently on the lawn, I'm windblown, a tiny bit sunburned, and riding a high like no other. I unbuckle the straps that held me in place through some pretty intense maneuvers, then slide down from Fabian's back and race forward to his head.

Or at least, that's what I intended to do. Unfortunately, after a couple hours in one position, my legs have different ideas, and my knees give way.

"Oops." I look up from where I'm sitting on the grass as Sophie strides toward me. "I think I might need a hand."

"Looks like," she says cheerfully. "Don't worry, it happens a lot. You just need a minute for your muscles to relax. Fabian, if you're going to move, go the other way."

Instead of moving, Fabian shifts back to his biped form and comes to sit on the grass beside me.

"We probably stayed up too long for your first time," he apologizes. "Did you have fun?"

"It was one of the most incredible experiences of my life, and I want to do it again and again… so many times." I massage the muscles in my thighs, trying to get them to wake up. Fabian pushes my hands away and takes over, and I flop back to lie in the grass and let my sexy… whatever he is rub me down.

"That feels good," I mumble.

"I'm starting to feel like a third wheel," Sophie declares, but that doesn't stop her from lying down beside me. "It's a lovely day, isn't it? I should try to get a flight in too." She doesn't move, though.

"You definitely should," I reply with my eyes closed. "Everything seems so much clearer up there. Air, thoughts…" Although now that I'm on the ground again, all my worries about our downhill slide into losing our abilities pile back in.

More to comfort myself than anything else, I open my eyes and pull from my sorcery. Not much, just enough for a tiny weave, something I taught myself as a child. Above me, a line of colorful, sparkling balls form, and I begin weaving them in patterns. Simple at first, then, as I remember how it's done, they become more intricate.

"Pretty," Sophie says. Fabian's stopped massaging me and is watching too.

"Thanks. It's just illusion, but it's always made me happy."

"Aren't most things illusions?" Fabian asks absently, his eyes on my display. "We build complex systems and societies that all hinge on the flimsiest beliefs and ideas."

Well, that killed my calm. I let the weaves dissolve and sit up as the balls disappear. "I'm rather fond of our systems and societies, thanks, and would rather not think about how easily they can fall apart." Especially since it seems one of them is. And it's not even a "flimsy idea." How can our innate abilities be waning?

"Sorry," Fabian says sheepishly, but I'm not paying attention.

"What could possibly be causing this? What could affect nearly every species this way?"

I don't have to explain what I'm talking about. It's been haunting all of us, even the dragons, who aren't directly impacted.

Sophie sighs and sits up also. "There are some poisons that can inhibit natural abilities," she offers. "I think there might even be one that does it for all species."

"Airborne? Waterborne? And capable of spreading through the whole world—and your world too—and poisoning every single one of us in increasing amounts over thousands of years?"

She shakes her head. "No. It's quite rare anyway, and it needs to be injected into the bloodstream."

"Hold on." Fabian's frowning. "What did you just say? About it needing to spread through our world too?"

Sophie and I exchange glances. Did he zone out in the middle of what I was saying?

"We were talking about it maybe being poison," Sophie explains patiently.

"No, I heard that. But how did it spread between worlds? There's been no contact between the worlds since your species wars."

I blink, turning that over in my mind. "You're sure? None at all?" They're better connected than me and have more information about this and how they came back to Earth. All I know is what was in the official statement—that elves and dragons had once been regular visitors to Earth, stopped during the species wars, but now faced the destruction of their homeworld and needed sanctuary, which the lucifer had offered them. Fabian's spoken a little about his home, but I haven't pressed. I can tell it hurts him to think about it, and I can't blame him for that. Even if I am wildly curious about what could cause the destruction of a whole planet like that.

Sophie and Fabian look at each other. "Weeeell," Sophie hedges. "There was some. But it was so minimal, the odds of something transferring randomly between planets are absurdly small."

"Besides," Fabian adds, "all signs point to this reduction in abilities happening within the same timeframe and at a similar pace on both worlds. If it started on one and then spread to the other, the second one should be lagging behind a lot more."

"And we still can't identify what 'it' is, anyway," I add reluctantly. "It would have to be a widespread environmental thing, right?"

"That's what I was getting at," Fabian interjects. "What's environmental on *both* worlds, widespread, that every species has contact with?"

"We all breathe oxygen. I don't know what the atmospheric makeup was on your planet, but it can't have been too different to here. I guess if there was a change to air quality, that could have an impact." I can hear my own doubt. Air quality isn't the same everywhere, and this issue has impacted evenly across the globe.

"No." Sophie shakes her head. "The air quality on our planet changed drastically over the last few thousand years. If it was that, the elves would have been affected much more dramatically."

Fabian's staring off into the distance, and I wonder if he's accessing the archive. "I feel like I've missed something," he murmurs. "It's important, but I just can't…"

Sighing, I haul myself to my feet. "It'll come back to you. Come on, let's go in. I'm starving, and I could murder a cup of coffee."

"That's a good idea. I think there was some of that custard thing left over from last night's dessert." Sophie holds up her hand. I grab it and pull her up, then reach down for Fabian. He accepts my help, but rather than letting go and stepping away as Sophie did, he wraps his arms around me and presses close.

"Hi," he says against my mouth.

I smile and let my eyes close as tingling pleasure drifts through me. "Hi. Thank you for today."

"I'm glad you enjoyed it. I had fun sharing it with you." He lays a kiss on the corner of my mouth, then lets me go and steps back... but takes my hand, the metal of his rings warm against my fingers.

As we walk up to the house, my mind whirls with the knowledge that it's officially too late for me to avoid heartbreak.

CHAPTER ELEVEN

Fabian

I LOOK around the conference room and wrinkle my nose. It's so boring. This is not the right location for me to share the wonders of dragon history and culture. We should be in a meadow somewhere, with lush grass and bold flowers… at the top of a cliff. Overlooking an ocean. And there should be a forest nearby.

But sadly, Percy said none of that was an option, so instead I'm in a conference room at the DEA offices. My first class about dragons is going to be to a test audience. Only a dozen people are coming, and they either work for CSG or have a family connection to someone who does. And Rhys's friend Sura. Apparently she begged him, and he was so awkward and embarrassed when he asked if it was okay that I would have given him anything. It's not a big deal, anyway.

Some have interacted with dragons before, and some have never met one. It should give me some excellent feedback on both content and my teaching method. I worked with the community archivists and Rhys and my friends on what I should be teaching, and we decided the first class would be a great "talk to a dragon" experience. Let people ask questions and determine what they most want to know before segueing into what I have planned. After all, dragons have been around for millions of years. I can't teach everything.

Before anyone arrives, though, I need to make this conference room more interesting. I just can't teach in here all day with it looking this way. I focus my magic and create an illusion, calling up a memory from when I was very young, back before the anomalies had destroyed too much of my home. I've just got it looking the way I want it when the conference room door swings open.

"Fabian, I thought I'd… Um. This isn't what I expected." Percy bites his lip to hide his smile. "Redecorating?"

I grin at him. Percy was the perfect addition to our family. He takes everything we do in stride, but still manages to steer us away from making poor choices. Mostly.

"Nobody could fully understand dragons while sitting in a four-walled box, Percy."

He glances around. "It's lovely. But honestly, Fabian, I don't think anyone who's not a dragon could ever fully understand dragons, no matter where they are."

I wave my hand dismissively, then get distracted by the way my rings catch the light. I've dressed up for today, with a ring on every finger, and they're so beautiful. There's my purity ring, of course, which I can't take off. I don't think I would even if I could. It links me to Rhys, a memory of our meeting and a symbol of our connection. Kethe was right all those months ago when she said I was different with him, and I was foolish to push that aside. I've always considered myself happy, content with my life and myself, and that was true, but being with Rhys has shown me how much more I can have. I've never been so simultaneously comfortable with and excited by anyone in my entire life.

Sometimes I think he knows me better than I do. It's not possible, of course, but take the ring I'm wearing on my pinky finger. The band is yellow, white, and rose gold woven together and set with a round yellow tourmaline. It's a ring I would have glanced past while shopping, but Rhys bought it for me last week and said the sight of it made him think of me. So of course I put it on. And the minute it was on my finger, I realized it was a ring I hadn't known I needed. It's so beautiful and suits me so well. I've barely taken it off since then.

"Fabian?"

Blinking, I return my attention to Percy, who has that patient look he gets when we're talking and I zone out. What were we talking about? Oh, right.

"You understand us just fine," I point out.

"That might be an overstatement." His voice is dry. "But I just came to see if you were ready, and it looks like you are. Do you need me for anything?"

I look around the room again. The illusion really is lovely. Rolling hills of orange grass lead to a distant horizon, scattered with small groves of tréghel trees. I've made it twilight, which shows off the glowing leaves on the trees. There are small patches of wildflowers to add even more beauty. A light breeze rustles among them.

"I think I'm good," I say confidently.

Percy smiles. "Have fun." He's chuckling to himself as he leaves.

A few minutes later, a cluster of five people come in. A few gasp when they see the illusion, and they all look around curiously.

"Hi! Welcome. Make yourselves comfortable, and we'll get started soon. I'm Fabian."

They introduce themselves and find seats, murmuring together and pointing to various things in my illusion.

"Excuse me, Fabian, is this your homeworld?" one of the men asks, a youngish vampire. He's very attractive, but I don't feel any urge to flirt. Okay, I do, but just casually. Not meaningfully. Flirting can be fun and doesn't always have to lead somewhere.

"Yes, it is. Not recently, though. The last time I saw this area in this condition was just under three thousand years ago. Give or take," I add, because I'm still not all that great at converting cycles to years. Math is gross.

"I think I've seen those glowing leaves before," someone else muses. "Doesn't David Carew wear one around his neck?"

"Yes," a new voice says, and I glance at the doorway, finding a familiar face.

"Hi, Noah." Noah works with the lucifer's team as an administrator, but he's got a keen interest in history, specifically human history within the community. He was the first person to truly rediscover the use of human magic, and he's also been to my homeworld. It wasn't a great visit for him, what with the kidnapping and fear for his life—not to mention the escape that nearly killed him—but it made him curious, and every time I've seen him, he's asked me questions about our heritage. I'm not surprised to see him here.

"Hey, Fabian."

It takes a few more minutes for everyone to arrive, but when they're all settled, I gently nudge the door closed with my magic and settle cross-legged on the conference table.

Some of them look surprised. Sura smiles. I need to make sure I get a chance to talk to her before she leaves.

"If you weren't here when I said it before, I'm Fabian Draco. I'm a dragon, and my job is to record and curate the lives and events of all dragons. Have any of you heard of the living archive?"

There are a few nods, some confused looks, and open curiosity. I quickly explain what the living archive is, then add, "So I have direct access to everything that's ever happened to any dragon not currently living. Anything you want to know about dragons"—I point both thumbs at my chest—"I'm your guy."

A chuckle goes around the table.

"What you see here," I wave at the illusion, "is a landscape that was fairly typical a few thousand years ago. It doesn't actually mean anything special, but I didn't like how the conference room looked, so you're all visiting the land of my childhood with me."

Another chuckle.

"It's been a long time since I've taught classes, and I've never been a fan of formality. So be comfortable, and let's kick off with some questions. What do you most want to know about dragons?"

Noah pulls out a list. I don't know him super well, but I'm still not surprised. Someone else speaks first, though, and just like that, my first dragon class begins.

"I DON'T UNDERSTAND," Koman, a demon with resting bitch face but a surprisingly pleasant manner, says. "You just didn't exist, and then one day you decided to be dragons?"

"No." I shake my head. "We existed. We just weren't corporeal. In much the same way as you won't be corporeal when this life ends and you move on to the spiritual plane. You can't exist here without your body, however, and we can. It's just a matter of changing our basic energy."

Noah snorts. "Oh, is that all? So simple."

I smile at him. "It really is."

"So, wait," Koman persists doggedly. "Are you, like, the same as the magic? Part of the energy that makes up everything?"

"Yes and no. It's hard to explain… like you, we're made up of the life force, what you call the magic. But unlike you, we directly siphon the life force for our magic. You draw from an inner well to channel your abilities. We never had one, because originally, we weren't corporeal. We just drew the energy we needed from whatever space we inhabited. When we chose to become corporeal, that stayed the same. It's why dragons are able to do things that aren't possible for elves or sorcerers—we have an infinite pool of energy to draw from, and we don't think the same way. In some ways, we exist outside the normal rules for other corporeal species, because originally we weren't supposed to be corporeal."

"Whoa," Noah mutters. "That's trippy."

Everyone laughs, and I grin. I'm thrilled with how well things are going so far.

By the time the end of the day rolls around, I'm completely energized. I haven't been able to engage in this kind of lively exchange of knowledge for so, so long, and seeing the excited and interested faces of my students as they absorbed what I was saying has been like sustenance for my soul. I can't wait to get home and tell Rhys all about it.

Sura lingers as the others filter out, coming to the front and perching beside me on the table. "Hey."

"Hey?" We've been in this room together all day. Aren't we past "hey"?

"This was a lot of fun. Thanks for letting me come."

I smile, remembering how red Rhys's face was when he asked and how relieved he was when I said yes. "I'd do anything for Rhys."

Her face lights up. "Really? Because he's got it bad for you, and I don't want to see him get hurt again."

My smile disappears. "Who hurt him?"

"People." She waves a hand. "Rhys is a shy science nerd with a big heart who wants to be loved. He gets attached very easily, and a lot of people haven't taken as much care with him as they should." She stares at me pointedly.

"I would never hurt Rhys," I snap. "Tell me who hurt him and I'll… I'll…" What's the worst thing I can do to them? "I'll tell Steffen they're a security risk!"

"You'll what?" Her expression clearly implies that I've lost my mind. "Look, I didn't say that you would hurt him deliberately. It's just… he's really in this. If you're not, maybe back off now, before he gets even more invested."

I can't believe Rhys's best friend thinks I could ever do anything to hurt him. "Are you trying to make me end things with him? What's *wrong* with you?"

"I'm not trying to make you end it," she declares. "Not if you really want to be with him. But if you're not as committed to this as he is, then—"

"Leave? Is that what you're saying? How can you be his best friend and not see how perfect he is?"

"I *do*. But other people don't, and he always gets his heart broken!" She throws up her hands in exasperation. "Look, Fabian, I like you. I think you're fun and really good for Rhys, who forgets to have fun. I *really* like how happy he is right now. If you can keep making him this happy, I'm going to be your friend for life, whether you want me to or not. But if you're not ready for a serious relationship, don't string him along."

I stare at her. "I think you should go." Does she do this with everyone Rhys dates? How many asshats have left because she scared them away? How can she not see that Rhys and I are supposed to be together? We fulfil each other's every need. She said herself that he's happy with me... that's because we make each other happy and always will.

I've never had this kind of relationship before, where one person is all I need, all I want. It's the most amazing thing I've ever experienced, and I'm not giving it up. I'm not giving Rhys up.

Sura sighs and gathers her things. "Just please look after him. He deserves to be worshiped by the man he's with."

"I do," I promise, relenting a little. "I know how special he is."

She leaves, and I spend a few moments worrying

about Rhys. He needs his best friend, and he needs me. If Sura doesn't want me in his life, then what happens?

A light knock at the door draws my attention, and I glance up to see Caolan standing in the doorway.

"Are you busy?" he asks.

I shake my head. "No, come in. I was just thinking."

He steps into the room and looks around at my illusion, faint pain crossing his features. "I sometimes forget how beautiful it was. The last years were so awful."

"I know. If you want, I can—"

"No, it's fine. It's nice to remember it, even if it hurts." He smiles wistfully. "I gave David a tréghel leaf for his birthday the first year we came here. It's silly, but every time I see it around his neck, I know where my home is."

I know what he means. Lately, I've been thinking about giving Rhys one of my rings. There's one I brought from home... it's the oldest ring I have, although not the first I ever hoarded, and it's so beautiful. It was crafted millennia ago and used to be one of a pair, handed down from loving couple to loving couple. The engraving on it reads "Alone I am only half, but with you I am whole."

When the troubles began on our homeworld, the second ring was lost, and the couple who'd owned them gave this one to me. They wanted a new matching set to show their bond but believed the ring should be preserved and cherished for what it is: an incredible piece of our history and a symbol of the love so many of our people have felt through the generations. When I look at it, I can't help but feel connected to my home and my people. And I want Rhys to wear it. Because he's woken up a part of me I didn't know I had, making me whole.

"Yes," I murmur, and Caolan smiles knowingly.

"That's actually what I came to talk to you about."

I blink. "Tréghel leaves?"

He laughs. "No. Relationships."

"Okay. Um. I'm not really the best person to ask for relationship advice." I might be loving the one I'm in, but it *is* my first, after all.

"That's okay. I'm not looking for advice. But I heard that things between you and Rhys are getting serious."

I narrow my eyes at him. "Did Sura put you up to this?" She might be Rhys's best friend, but I know enough about history to know the divisive, conniving gossip needs to be ended before they can start a war.

Although neither Rhys nor I have armies at our command, so that's probably not going to be an issue.

"Who's Sura?" Caolan asks in confusion.

"Never mind," I sigh. He studies me for a moment.

"I rarely do this," he admits finally. "Not unless I'm asked. But Percy is David's best friend, and since he and Brandt got together, that means David's kind of adopted you dragons too. Because Percy loves you and David would do anything for Percy. So that means I have a vested interest in seeing you all happy."

"I'm happy. Why would you think I'm not? I'm a ray of sunshine."

He shakes his head. "No, that's not what I meant. I… This is about you and Rhys."

"If you're about to suggest that I should break up with Rhys, you need to stop talking right now and back away before I search the archives for a spell that would turn your skin inside out," I warn.

Surprisingly, a grin breaks over his face. "I'm not," he assures me. "I'm not doing this right, and I'm sorry for that. Did you know that I can see paired souls?"

The question hangs in the air between us.

"I didn't," I say around the sudden lump in my throat. "Are you asking me if I'm serious about Rhys because he and I are paired or because we're not?"

"I won't answer that unless you want to know."

I feel like I can't breathe. "A relationship can be loving and important and meaningful even if the couple's souls aren't paired," I say.

"Of course. Most relationships are like that." He shakes his head again, his silvery blond hair sliding over his shoulder.

"Even if Rhys and I aren't paired souls, that doesn't mean I'd love him any less or that what we have means any less. That we won't still be together always." I know this. I'm an academic. I know this intellectually and right down to the very essence of my being. But that doesn't mean I don't want Caolan to tell me our souls are paired.

He says nothing, watching me, waiting for me to decide.

Will this make a difference to me? To how I feel about Rhys?

"I don't need to know," I tell Caolan firmly. "I love Rhys, and that's not going to change."

The grin returns. "It's really not going to change," he says. "Not ever."

I suck in a deep breath, hope exploding inside me despite my resolution that it didn't matter. "You mean we are?"

He nods. "I saw it the minute I met him. It shines from you both so brightly."

"Wow." I rest my hands on the surface of the table for balance, even though I'm sitting. "This really is forever."

"If you want it to be."

I look him in the eye. "I've never wanted anything more."

CHAPTER TWELVE

Rhys

FABIAN CAME HOME from his first day teaching in an odd mood. He seemed almost jubilant, and my first thought was that it must be about how his class went, but when I asked him about the class, his manner changed. He was still happy and excited, pleased with the way the day went, but that edge of giddiness was gone.

Who knows? I've given up trying to fully understand dragons. Accepting Fabian for who he is makes me happy.

That doesn't mean I'm not still wondering about it the next day. I check on the grad students I've hired to assist me in the lab, look at the latest data, and sit through a Zoom meeting with Imani and the others, but in the back of my mind, I'm still wondering what made Fabian so elated last night.

And also what's making Sura so weird today.

She's been watching me all morning. Every time we're in the same room, I feel her gaze on me, and when I look up, she's got this tense expression on her face. I've asked her twice already if she's okay, and she just smiles brightly and says "Sure!" which is just more evidence that she's not. Sura is not a bright-smile type of person. She's an eye-roll, sarcastic-reply type of person.

It's lunchtime before I have time to corner her. "Let's eat out!" I announce, grabbing her arm and pulling her up from her desk chair.

"I brought lunch," she protests.

I level her with *the look*. The one that says "who are you and what have you done with my friend of sixty years?" Because Sura never passes up the chance to have lunch out.

She sighs. "Fiiiine. Let me grab my wallet."

Ten minutes later, we've nabbed the last table at the noodle place two blocks from KRD, and I go up to order while Sura glares menacingly at the people who wanted it but weren't fast enough.

"So," I say when I've deposited our drinks and order ticket on the table and settled into my chair. "Are you going to tell me what's going on with you?"

"There's nothing going on with me. I'm fine. It's fine."

"Seriously?" She can't really think I believe her, right?

"Let's just change the subject." She glances around desperately, opening her bottle of Sprite. "Nice weather we're having lately."

I snort. "Fine, we'll change the subject. But we can do better than the weather. Did you have fun yesterday in Fabian's class?"

She chokes on her soda and sprays liquid over the table. Fortunately, none of it reaches me. I hand her a napkin.

"Nothing's going on, huh?"

Avoiding my eyes, she mops herself and the table up. "Sura—"

Our ticket number is called at that precise moment, and she leaps from her chair. "I'll get it!"

Sighing, I let her go. I need to think anyway. Did something happen yesterday? Wouldn't Fabian have mentioned it if there was weirdness with Sura? Unless he vagued out… or doesn't know.

What if Sura doesn't like Fabian?

My stomach sinks like a stone. That would be so bad, if my best friend and the guy I'm hoping will one day be my boyfriend don't like each other. Especially since Sura's a pretty blunt person. What if Fabian guesses that she doesn't like him and it influences any decision he might make about being with me?

The thought is beneath me, but I can't help letting it get its claws into my brain.

Sura places a heaping plate of Pad Thai in front of me, then sits with her own. "This smells great," she declares with too much enthusiasm.

"Do you hate Fabian?" I blurt.

Her chopsticks clatter to the tabletop.

"You do," I moan. "You hate him."

"I don't hate him," she says slowly, picking up the chopsticks and studying them. "Why would you think that?"

"Sura."

"I really don't," she assures me. "I actually like him a lot." She hesitates. "He might not like me so much, though."

"Why?" If someone had asked me, I would have said the two of them would get along like a house on fire.

She puts down the chopsticks and looks me in the eye. "I might have given him the best friend speech."

My eyes widen in panic. "You did *what*?"

"I just don't want to see you get hurt again. I needed to make sure he understands how amazing you are," she babbles, holding up her hands as though to fend me off.

"I'm not even sure if he wants to be in a committed relationship, and you're giving him the talk as though he's my boyfriend?" I think I might actually die. "Why would you do this to me?"

She points at me. "This is why! You're so far gone over him, but he won't even commit to being with you. I hate that you're being made to feel so insecure, and I just wanted him to see that you're worth committing to. You'd be the best boyfriend he's ever had."

I suck in oxygen, wondering if it's possible for my airways to close just from stress. "What did he say?" Fabian was in a good mood last night and gave no indication he wanted to end things, but that doesn't mean anything. Maybe he just wanted another casual night of fucking before he left me forever. Maybe he was happy because he was thinking of all the other men he could be with once he walked away from me.

Sura shakes her head. "He… lectured me on not knowing how special you are? I'm not really clear what happened, but he wasn't happy with me."

I shove my noodles away and plant my elbows on the table so I can bury my face in my hands. "What does that mean?" I moan.

"What? I can't hear you with your hands over your face like that."

Unburying myself, I glare at her. "Don't be a smart-ass, Sura. This is all your fault."

"I'm sorry! I just don't want you to get hurt. I waited all last night for you to call me because he said something. I barely slept!"

"Good," I snap viciously. "I hope you get bags under your eyes."

The women at the next table gasp, and I look over to see them staring at me with shocked expressions.

"She gave the guy I'm *casually dating* the best friend speech," I say, and the shock turns to understanding.

"Oh, honey, no," one of them says to Sura with a pitying shake of the head.

"Thank you! See?" I tell my best friend, and then as the women turn back to their own conversation, I add in a whisper, "Even the humans get it."

Sura sniffs but nods. "I know I was wrong, and I'm sorry. But he clearly didn't let it bother him that much if he never said anything to you about it. Was he weird or anything? Weirder," she adds, and I don't even have the heart to scold her for the implication that Fabian's weird.

"He was," I concede, "but not in a bad way? He was happy. Really happy. Maybe because he's planning to never see me, and by extension you, ever again." I pick up my chopsticks and poke my noodles. Not even Pad Thai can make me feel better right now.

Though it does smell amazing.

"If he was that happy at the thought of leaving you, why would he have even gone back to your place last night? He could have gone anywhere else. And he seemed into you. I'm still not sure how the conversation got turned around, but he definitely wasn't pleased at the thought that I was undervaluing you… I think." She points at my plate. "Eat. You need your strength to think clearly."

Reluctantly, I dig into my noodles, trying to rationalize with myself. This is why I've been avoiding dating for the past few… decades. It's hard, and it hurts when I get more invested than the guy I'm with. I don't want to be the pathetic man who takes whatever scraps he can get. I want to be with someone who's entirely committed to me and wants me just as much as I do him. Is that too much to ask?

I sigh, ignore Sura's searching look, and shove noodles and tofu into my mouth. Fabian hasn't given any indication he's ready to walk away… or that he wants to. Sure, he's never spoken about us being more than casual, but I'm sure he hasn't been with anyone else, and he's not grudging with his company. We spend a lot of time together, and he's happy about it. He initiates it. So whatever it is we have, it's not me trapping him in a situation he doesn't want.

The problem right now isn't Fabian. It's me. My insecurities. I want certainty, but I'm scared that if I ask Fabian for a commitment, or even just to define our relationship, he'll back away. That's on me: I'm not prepared to take the risk, so I need to live with the uncertainty.

I can do that, because what I have with Fabian right now is so much better than not having him at all.

When I get home, I'm surprised to find Fabian there, almost bouncing in excitement over something. This morning he told me he had to go back to Here Be

Dragons today, and I expected him to stay there tonight. I guess it's a good sign that he chose to come back instead and is seemingly very happy to see me.

Believe in yourself. You are worthy of love.

I'm not sure where those thoughts come from, but as far as mantras go, they suck. I'm a scientist. I need evidence, thanks, not just empty phrases of reassurance.

"You're home!" Fabian grins widely and bounces over to kiss me. "I have something for you."

"You do?" I manage to dump my laptop bag before he grabs my hand and drags me to the bedroom. "Ohhhh. You have *something* for me." I'm not going to complain. My sex drive might have been in hibernation before, but Fabian well and truly dusted it off, tuned it up, and has it constantly wanting more.

"That, too, but after. Sit." He nudges me toward the bed, and I obediently go and sit. For a moment, he studies me. "You should probably be naked."

I start to smile. "I thought that was happening after?"

Gesturing impatiently, he comes to stand beside me and begins unbuttoning my shirt. "It is. But you're beautiful naked, and I think that will show it off to the best effect."

Relenting, I stand and take over stripping myself. "I have no idea what you're talking about, but I'm not going to skip a chance to be naked with you. So you need to take your clothes off too."

He shrugs and yanks his T-shirt over his head. Fabian has zero body issues and only wears clothes to protect his sensitive bits and because it's the law. Dragons can regulate their own body temperature, so it's not like he needs them to stay warm.

In less than a minute, we're both naked, and I sit patiently back on the bed and wait for whatever he wants to give me. Then I'll jump him, and after we've fucked each other into a sweaty stupor, we can order takeout for dinner and eat it in bed.

This may be one of the best plans I've ever made.

He goes over to the overnight bag in the corner and bends to dig into a side pocket. The view makes my cock perk up, and I sigh happily. When he finally straightens and turns around, he doesn't even seem to realize what a lovely show he gave me.

"Here." He crosses the room to sit beside me on the bed, a small bundle wrapped in black velvet in his hand. I reach for it, but he draws it back and unfolds the fabric himself, revealing a wide silver ring.

I'm still blinking at it in surprise when he takes my right hand and threads it onto my forefinger. The band covers most of the space between my first and second knuckles and is intricately carved with what looks like words, but in a language I don't recognize.

"It's… gorgeous," I say. The word feels lacking. There's something about this ring that's *more*. "Are those words? What do they say?" And what does it mean that he's putting it on my finger? Is this a commitment, dragon-style? But Percy and Rob don't wear rings, and Brandt and Dustin are two of the most committed people I've ever met.

Fabian is smiling at the ring on my finger. "It's an old engraving. This ring has been around for longer than I've been alive."

Whoa. I look at it with new eyes.

"This is an antique then." Majorly antique. It should be in a museum, and that's even before you factor in that it's an artifact from a now-destroyed dimension.

Fabian laughs and lifts my hand to kiss my knuckle, right above the ring. "It is. Even for us." He keeps hold of my hand, studying it and smiling still.

This is starting to freak me out. "Is, uh, is this from your hoard? Should it even be worn?" My hands are bigger than Fabian's, and it fits my forefinger perfectly. I guess it would maybe fit his thumb, but the band's too wide for that to be comfortable. Does that mean he hoards rings he can't wear? I have so many questions about his hoard, but he doesn't talk about it a lot. He changes his rings—aside from the one for the study, of course—almost every day, and I like to compliment him on them because I know it's important to him, but he never says a lot about them.

"It was made to be worn," he assures me. "I like seeing it on you. Your fingers are always so bare. I think I'll start bringing you rings to wear more often."

My stomach sinks. So this is like a decorative loan?

I summon a smile. "Thank you. I… uh, don't wear rings much, though." Or at all.

"Let's start with this one for now. It's the perfect adornment for you." His gaze finally skims away from the ring to the rest of me. "Oh, yes."

My disappointment falls away. It's impossible to miss the appreciation in Fabian's tone, and he really did make a big deal about me wearing this ring. It has to mean something, if only that he considers me an important part of his life. And even if it doesn't mean anything, I still get to be with him.

Lying back on the bed, I put my left hand behind my head and flex, watching as Fabian's eyes glaze over.

"Mm, yes," he murmurs. "The perfect adornment."

I run the hand with the ring on it over my abs and down to my semi-erect cock, taking a firm hold and giving myself a few strokes.

He grins and climbs up on the bed to straddle my thighs. "I want to play with that. Share."

Chuckling, I keep half-heartedly jacking myself. "I don't know. It's one of my favorite toys. Are you going to take good care of it?"

Not bothering to respond verbally, he leans over and licks the head, and I gasp.

"Okay, you can have a turn."

His grin turns smug. "Both hands above your head," he orders. A shiver goes through me, and I obey. The headboard is solid, so I just clasp my hands together. I'm pretty sure I'll need to be holding on to something.

Next, he kneels up, thighs spread wide, and conjures some of his magic lube. I love that stuff. Not only does it feel great, but I never have to worry about being caught without.

"Eyes on me," he demands, then proceeds to prep himself.

I go hard as a spike. Fabian and I are both vers, and I have topped him a few times, but mostly we both prefer when he's being dominant in the bedroom. I don't know why it never occurred to me that this is the obvious solution. My sex drought was clearly far too long.

I watch greedily. From this angle, I can't see exactly what his hand is doing, but Fabian wears everything he's feeling on his face, and the shift of expressions is enough to tell the full story.

Swallowing hard, I let my gaze drop to his cock. It's

semihard and pointing toward me, long and flushed, the light casting fascinating shadows amongst the ridges and dips of it.

"Fabian," I gasp, squeezing my hands together. His eyes focus on me, and that wicked smile is back.

"Look at you, waiting so patiently," he praises, shuffling forward. My dick brushes against his inner thigh, and I suck in a breath. "Let me get started, and then you can help."

Oh, yeah. I bite my lip, and his gaze catches there.

"But first, I need a taste." He leans down, pressing the length of his torso against mine, our cocks rubbing together, and kisses me deeply, hot and wet.

Then pulls away.

The noise of protest I make catches in my throat as he raises himself again, then takes hold of my dick and slowly lowers onto it.

Yesssssss.

"How can anything feel this good?" I gasp as he bottoms out and rocks back and forth in tiny increments, settling in.

"I ask myself that every time I'm with you," he replies, and my body reacts as though to a touch. "Give me your hand."

I obey instinctively, releasing the death grip I have on my own hands and bringing the right one forward to offer him. He takes it, smearing lube on my fingers, and closes it around his cock. I tighten my grip reflexively, loving the way he shudders.

Then I notice the ring still on my finger.

"Wait, let me swap hands." I don't want to hurt him.

"Don't you dare," he chides. "Try to keep the rhythm."

Before I can ask what he means, he rises, causing my eyes to roll back in my head and my hold on him to shift. Okay. I get it now.

I jerk him off as he fucks himself on me, my eyes glued to him the whole time. I've never met anyone like him, so casually confident and secure in themselves. His face is flushed with arousal, sweat beading on his skin—which I've learned is a true sign of how into it he is. He's forgotten to regulate his body temperature. The heady sensation of power floods through me, and my balls draw up tight.

"Gonna come," I manage, and he opens his eyes.

"Do it. Fill me up."

The words are all I need.

I'm still coming when he tightens around me, his muscles contracting on my cock, and I force my eyes open to watch his orgasm even as I gasp for breath. His head is thrown back, his spine arched. There's no cum, of course—dragons don't produce any, something that fascinated me when I first learned it. Now, all I can think is how beautiful he is like this.

Finally, panting, our bodies relax. Fabian eases off my dick and lays his body over mine, snuggling close. I wrap my arms around him, and the glint of the ring he put on my finger catches my eye.

It has to mean something.

CHAPTER THIRTEEN

Rhys

I PACE across my kitchen floor, hands gripping my hair, trying desperately to work out what I'm missing. What we're all missing. This isn't even my job, but I can't let it go. *Something* is causing our natural abilities to slowly reduce. Why can't any of us work out what it is?

I've known about this problem for six months. Others have been working on it for years. We're all intelligent; some of them are the best in their respective fields. We have resources at our disposal. We're thinking outside the box. So why can't any of us work out this problem?

Are we not supposed to?

That's the thought that has me awake at three in the morning, that pulled me from my warm bed and the warmer dragon sleeping there. Maybe we're not meant to solve this. Maybe the magic has determined, for whatever reason, that we're supposed to slowly die out… or become human. Is that even possible? As a sorcerer, there are fewer obvious differences between me and an average human than there would be if I was a shifter or a vampire, for example. We look mostly the same. Our bodies don't change. The only true difference is my well of internal power and the ability to weave it. If that well was gone, the weaves forgotten… would I still be a sorcerer?

I want to say yes. I've never considered myself xenophobic, but maybe I am, because the thought of being human—or anything other than a sorcerer—is completely anathema to me. My sorcery is part of who I am.

But if this is some form of evolution, there's nothing we can do to change it. Is there? I wish there was a way to know. It's said that our species leaders and the lucifer can communicate with the magic, but I'm not sure this theory is something I want to share with anyone. And what happens if the magic confirms it? Maybe I don't want to know after all.

"What are you doing?"

I turn to where Fabian is blinking sleepily in the doorway.

"Did I wake you? I'm sorry." I go to him and wrap him in my arms. The comfort of having him pressed against me is beyond my ability to describe.

He snakes his arms around my waist and turns his face into my neck, planting a kiss there. "What's wrong?"

"Nothing. I—I'm sorry I woke you." I so desperately want to share my fears with him, but I can't. I don't want to scare him off.

"Missing you in bed woke me," he corrects, his voice muffled against my skin. "But you're clearly too upset about something to sleep, so the only way to resolve this is for you to tell me what the problem is so I can help you fix it."

My arms tighten reflexively. He kisses my neck again, then slips free, taking my hand and leading me to the kitchen table.

"Sit," he orders, patting the back of a chair. "I'll make some tea, and you can tell me all about it."

"I don't want tea," I protest weakly, sitting in the chair. He takes the one beside me.

"Then I won't make any."

We sit in silence. I can't quite bring myself to speak and let him see exactly how neurotic I am. This time with him has been so wonderful, has lasted so much longer than I expected, and I can't quite bring myself to ruin that. I want him for as long as I can have him.

"Rhys," he prompts, and I sigh.

"It's stupid. I keep thinking about work… about our abilities decreasing."

He frowns, frustration in his eyes. He's been searching the living archive in every spare moment for information that might help, but it's hard when we don't know what we're looking for. "I get it," he says. "I know this has been weighing on you. But you need sleep."

I let my gaze drift down to where my hands are clasped on the tabletop, to the wide silver ring on my index finger. Fabian put it there weeks ago, but unlike the other rings he occasionally brings me to wear, he hasn't taken it back. I can't bring myself to take it off, not even when I'm sleeping. It's a tie to him that I don't want to let go of.

His hand covers mine now. "Rhys."

I sigh. "Who would I be without my sorcery?"

"You'd still be you," he says swiftly. "Self is not

defined by ability. You'd still be a scientist. Still be sweet and kind and socially awkward and a loner."

"Thanks." It's true, but that doesn't make it fun to hear.

He chuckles. "Why are you borrowing trouble like this? At the current rate of deterioration, you'll be long dead before complete loss is an issue."

"I know." I don't say anything else. He's right, of course. But…

After a moment, he adds, "Let's go over it again. When did the deterioration start?"

"It's hard to tell for sure, but we think about eight and a half thousand years ago. Records from before then are too patchy for us to be sure it wasn't already happening, but we think it wasn't."

"Why were records patchy? You had an established government then, right? I wasn't alive, but I know a lot of dragons and elves were visiting before that, and all our records speak of the lucifer." His fingers twitch, as though he wants to go check the archive, and I smile.

"Ah, we did. But a lot of information was destroyed during the species wars, and back then we didn't have a cloud backup like we do now."

He nods. "The species wars were, what, right around the time this started?"

"A bit before," I correct. "As near as we can tell, the wars had been over for a few hundred years when the deterioration began." I shake my head. "You're thinking the wars were a trigger. We've considered that too. But how?"

Fabian stares off into the distance. "I'm not sure. It obviously wasn't some kind of biological weapon."

"No," I say dryly. "No such thing existed back then.

Definitely nothing that would alter us so permanently. If we'd been fighting anyone but humans, I'd consider a slow-acting weave or spell. Or," I add with a laugh, "if we wanted to explore the realm of fantasy, a curse. But everyone knows curses don't exist."

He lifts a hand, index finger pointing up. "Hold on. Let's think about that."

"A *curse*?" Has he lost his mind? "Fabian—"

"No, no." He waves dismissively. "Not a curse."

I mentally rewind. "A weave, then? I was only kidding. No sorcerer would ever have done something like that to us all. And even if they did, it would be impossible to design such a weave. When you consider all the factors, the number of species it needs to affect, the amount of time we're talking about… it would have needed to be able to bond to the DNA of people who wouldn't be born for thousands of years. Changes in environment, evolution, crossbreeding between species… all things that couldn't be fully accounted for ahead of time. Someone might have tried, but even the best outcome would have it starting to fall apart within a thousand years. And the outcome definitely wouldn't be so even. It would work faster within some families and species than others. Plus, once we started looking, we'd be able to see the residue. No, it's definitely not a weave."

"What about a spell, then?" His eyes are still unfocused in the way they get when he's searching the archive.

"You think a dragon or elf did this?" I can't keep the incredulity from my voice. "Why, though? You all retreated back to your world when the war broke out. From what I've heard, there weren't any dragons or elves left here on Earth. If one or two did get left behind somehow, why would they side with humans, who were the aggressors?"

"No, I think the—" He stops so suddenly, it takes me a moment to realize he's not going to finish the sentence.

"Fabian?" I prompt. He's frowning, and his eyes are focused again.

"I'm going to tell you something, but you need to keep it to yourself. Only a very small percentage of the community knows this."

Apprehension coils in my stomach. "Should you be telling me, then?" I don't want him to get into trouble.

He hesitates. "I think so. I don't think you'll freak out. And maybe it will help. You know Noah?"

Blinking, I try to put his question into context. "Noah… you mean Noah who works at CSG? I've spoken to him a few times." He's David's liaison with the team working on this problem and my source for most of the historical data we've been using. He's human, which initially surprised me, but I've seen demons cower at the thought of having to ask him for something.

"Yes. There's a very long and complicated backstory that's highly classified, but what it comes down to is that Noah can use magic."

My jaw drops. "Shut the fuck up," I whisper. "Noah's… what? An elf? Surely not a dragon?" My mind spins a complex origin story wherein Noah is the last scion of an ancient elf who impregnated a human before leaving Earth thousands of years ago.

What? It could happen.

From the way Fabian's laughing, probably not, though.

"No," he gasps. "Noah's human. Very human."

I grin somewhat sheepishly, then frown. What does he mean, th—

I leap to my feet, knocking my chair over. "Humans can use spell craft?" This is a catastrophe!

Fabian leaps up also, taking my hand. "Please be calm and let me explain."

Unable to help myself, I reach out mentally and check the wards around the house. I'm not the best at weaving wards, but I've practiced these basic ones so often, it would be hard to fuck them up. They should keep out anyone uninvited, and if they fail will at least give me warning of an intruder. It gives me chills to think of humans using spells. They came so close to destroying us during the species wars. If not for the magic intervening to save us and wipe all memory of us from humanity, the community would have become extinct. If they'd had spell craft back then…

But wait…

I right my chair and collapse into it. "Did they have spell craft during the species wars?" I croak.

Fabian settles beside me and holds my hand firmly. "From what I understand, yes. That's what led the life force to intervene—they were abusing their magic to annihilate the other species."

I try not to think about that too hard. I have human neighbors, and I've always thought they were lovely people. Right now, though, I really wish I lived in an all-community neighborhood. What if some of them are like Noah and have rediscovered the use of spell craft? What if they're not that much like Noah, and instead want to finish what their long-ago ancestors started and wipe the community from the face of the Earth?

Fabian's watching me closely, and I muster up a

smile. Well… a grimace. I need to pull it together. "Can you tell me what happened? Did they… forget they had spell craft when they forgot about us? Did we forget too?"

He shrugs. "They were made to forget by the life force. I think the community just lost the knowledge over time, the same as it lost the knowledge about us. Since humans were no longer using magic, there was no need for anyone to think about it. CSG has records about it. Apparently there are some humans who still use it in minor ways… Wickers?"

I stare at him blankly. Is he saying humans use it to make furniture?

"It's some kind of religion," he persists. "They get naked under the moon."

"Ohhhh, Wiccans. Yeah, that makes sense. Although their religion is more complex than just getting naked," I feel compelled to add, even though I don't know a lot about it. But surely it must be, or there would be a lot more Wiccans.

Fabian purses his lips. "I should look into that. Human religions are fascinating. They've built these amazingly complex fictions and put so much energy into maintaining them."

"Another time, maybe. You were telling me how humans rediscovered spell craft."

He nods. "I don't know all the details. You should ask Noah. All I know is that some humans were using magic in a far reduced capacity, and then Noah came along and started learning to use it properly. He's mostly self-taught, since until we returned to Earth, there was limited information available. The elves have been able to help him with some things, and others he's puzzled out. He really has a remarkable mind, especially given how young he is. Did you—" He catches sight of my expression, which, if it reflects my mood, is not showing interest and enjoyment. "Anyway," he hurries on, "CSG made the decision—with the DEA's agreement—that at this stage, knowledge of human magic should be kept limited. They wanted to avoid widespread panic in the community and the possibility that someone would consider a preemptive strike against humans."

Shame fills me. Sure, I hadn't started planning to attack my neighbors, but is checking the wards and mentally planning to move elsewhere that much better? What have my neighbors ever done to make me think they might try to hurt me?

I guess the lucifer and his team made the right decision to keep this quiet.

"That's wise," I manage. "So... who knows?"

Fabian's mind has changed tacks, though. He's playing with the ring on my finger, a dreamy smile on his face. "This suits you so well. I knew it would. You're the only person I could ever have given it to."

As sweet as that is... "Fabian, who knows that humans can use spell craft?"

"Hmm?" He drags his gaze away from the ring. "Oh. Um... some people at CSG. A lot of the dragons and elves, of course. And most of the community members and humans who've intermarried."

That's another shock. Is CSG encouraging humans to use spell craft? There's always been a small number of community-human relationships. We live completely among them, after all, and it's foolish to think there can be separation. It sometimes gets tricky, but for the most part, we're cautious enough that the humans we welcome into the community become truly part of it. Still, what reason is there to teach them spell craft?

My conscience kicks me again. I've just said these humans are part of our community, but yet I'd deny them the chance to rediscover their own heritage?

I take a deep breath and try to shake off my inbuilt prejudices. "That's nice. I suppose those are the humans we can trust with it."

Fabian shrugs. "Maybe. But I think the reason they decided to do it was so those marriages didn't have to end so soon. It can't be easy to know you're going to outlive your spouse by hundreds of years."

He's right, of— Wait. "What?"

Blinking up at me in that way that makes him look so innocent, even though I know he's far from it, Fabian says, "What, what?"

"Are you saying human spellcasting can extend their lifespan?" That's... wow. It makes sense, though. The rest of the species all have longer lifespans, presumably connected to our abilities. Why shouldn't the human lifespan be connected to theirs... or the lack thereof?

He nods. "It's the same spell the elves use. A simple trick to freeze ageing. The lucifer thought it was cruel to prevent loved ones from being together, so the information has been quietly shared with those who would need it. The need for secrecy has been impressed upon them, of course."

I shake my head. "Of course. I just... wow. I think I might need some time to process this." I can't quite get my head around it. "I swear I won't tell anyone," I add. The sensitivity of the information aside, I wouldn't want to get Fabian in trouble. "Does this mean Rob knows? Since he and Dustin are together." I hope so. That's something that's made me sad a time or two, seeing them together and knowing that they likely only have another forty or fifty years.

"Oh yes. It was this whole big deal… I don't remember why. But he's been getting private lessons from Noah and is quite adept at magic now." He claps his hands. "Oh, he can show you! It's been tough for him keeping it a secret when you're around. He likes to show off."

This time, it's not shame I need to push away, but instead disappointment. I thought Fabian's family had accepted me, if not as one of their own, at least as someone they liked and trusted. Instead, I've been left out of the loop this whole time. I know Fabian and I probably aren't forever, but after six months of weekends spent at Here Be Dragons, I thought I was at least temporarily part of the group.

"What's wrong?" Fabian asks, startling me. He's perceptive in a lot of ways, but not usually when it comes to people's feelings.

"Nothing," I deny. "I-I'm just shocked, I guess. I never expected to be told this. Uh, why did you tell me?" I can't even remember how we got onto this topic.

Neither can Fabian, if the way he furrows his brow is any indication. Giving in to temptation, I lean over and kiss the puckered skin, and it smooths as his frown turns into a delighted smile.

"Ready to go back to bed?"

In response, I stand and draw him to his feet, pausing to kiss him before I lead the way toward the door. He skips along happily behind me, then stops abruptly in the doorway.

I glance back over my shoulder. "What?"

"I remember why I told you. We were talking about the possibility of a spell causing the deterioration of abilities…"

Never before have I actually felt the blood draining from my face. "Fuck. If the humans had spell craft…" Could this issue be the result of a spell the humans cast in an effort to annihilate us back then? I force myself to think rationally and without prejudice. "But they were trying to kill us. Every story I've heard says that. We were on the verge of extinction before the magic stepped in. Why would they have crafted such a slow-acting spell when they were so close to wiping us out anyway?"

Fabian shrugs, lips pursed. "I don't know. And I'm not even sure if their magic is capable of that kind of thing. We should talk to Noah." He pats his hip, then looks around. "Where's my phone?"

A chuckle escapes me, and I kiss him again. How did I get so lucky as to find him? "You're not calling Noah in the middle of the night. We'll talk to him in the morning." Part of me really wants answers, but my rational side knows this isn't an emergency.

My curious dragon disagrees. "But—"

"Bed," I remind him. "With me."

"You're wearing too many clothes" is his immediate reply as he slides his fingers into the waistband of my boxers. I capture his hand and use it to tug him along to the bedroom.

FOR THE FIRST TIME EVER, Fabian's already up when I wake the next morning. He's woken before me in the past, but he always stays in bed for a cuddle. Today, he's awake, out of bed, and fully dressed.

It's shocking.

"Are you okay?" I ask, frowning as I sit up. The covers slide to my lap, and I'm gratified by the way he freezes midmotion to look at my chest.

"Good morning, nipples," he says dreamily.

Okay, then.

"Fabian?" I take the cup of coffee he was midway to handing me. "Why have you brought me coffee in bed? Why are you even up? You don't have classes today." That's why he spent the night.

"Shh. I'm busy." He picks up my free hand and places the palm against my chest, right between my pecs, then adjusts my fingers so they're splayed. I look down at myself.

"Fabian, what are you doing?"

"So pretty," he breathes. "I'm going to get you a ring for every finger." He lightly strokes the ring I'm wearing. I nearly brained myself with it during the night, but I can't bring myself to take it off. Not when he put it there. Although I might have to draw the line at a ring on every finger. "I need a photo!" he announces, yanking his phone from his pocket.

"Of what?" And why am I still sitting here with my hand on my chest? I start to lift it away, but the sound of distress Fabian makes gives me pause. He's aiming his phone camera and a pleading expression at me. "You're joking."

"Please? The ring and your chest are the best jerkoff material ever. It's an instant boner."

I have no idea what to say to that, but I can't resist

him, so I leave my hand where he put it and let him take his photo.

"Nobody had better see that," I warn, though I guess it's not a big deal if they do. It's only my chest, after all. But it still feels like a private thing, just for Fabian.

He clutches the phone to his chest. "Never! I'm not sharing you."

Sighing, I lean back into the pillows and take a sip of my coffee. "So… why are you up and about so early?"

He climbs onto the mattress and sits cross-legged, watching me with a fond smile. "We need to talk to Noah this morning, remember? This is important to you. I wasn't going to lie in bed all day."

For a second, I can't breathe. It's a small thing, but he still put me before his own wants without me even having to mention it.

"Thank you," I manage. "Let me just finish my coffee, and I'll get ready."

"No rush," he says. "I called Noah already, and he said he'll stop by on his way to work. So you have"—he glances at his phone—"about an hour to get dressed."

"Did you tell him what it's about?" He must have— why else would Noah agree to come over? But Fabian shakes his head.

"I just said we had a theory that we wanted his input on." He reaches out to take my hand, fiddling with the ring while I sip my coffee. There's something intensely intimate about this moment, and my heart sings with it. I turn my hand in his and weave our fingers together, and Fabian's breath catches. The smile he gives me is… perfect.

"So you think humans might have used magic to slowly wipe out the community?" Noah shakes his head. "Fucking hell."

"It's just a theory," I rush to say. "I don't really think it fits, because why would they use such a slow-acting spell when they were so close to winning anyway? But I don't know enough about human spell craft or what actually happened back then to be sure." I hesitate. "I hope you're not offended."

He snorts. "On behalf of humanity? Nah. I can't dispute that we're a fucked-up species and capable of doing something so despicable. Some of us, anyway." He accepts the mug Fabian hands him. "Thanks. But I don't think it would be possible."

Fabian takes a seat beside me at the kitchen table. "Magically not possible?"

Noah shrugs. "I'm still learning the boundaries of human magic, but essentially, it's wish fulfilment. Where you sorcerers have to understand exactly what you're trying to do and design a weave to do it, I just have to draw on the magic and tell it what I want. It can be a bit more complex with some things, but that's the basis of it."

I try to make sense of that. "Wait… when you say you draw on the magic, do you mean *the* magic? What the dragons call the life force? The energy that makes up everything?"

He nods. "Yep. That's the difference between sorcery and human magic. You use your own inner power. I borrow from… well, the universe, I guess."

Something nags at the back of my mind, but I can't

quite place it. "Given the infinite amount of power available, wouldn't that make it even easier to implement this kind of spell?"

He sips his coffee. "Theoretically, maybe. But the magic itself won't allow it. The whole reason humans forgot they had this ability was because the magic realized what they were using it for and stepped in to protect the other species. We might not understand what motivates the essence of existence, but it clearly has a thing about mass genocide. Twice that we know of, it's acted to rescue whole species."

"Twice?" Fabian zones in instantly. "When was the other time?"

I raise an inquiring eyebrow, wondering the same thing. Has CSG found records from before the species wars?

Noah smirks. "You're here, aren't you?"

Sitting back, I consider that while Fabian sputters. "You think the dragons and elves coming to Earth was because the magic stepped in to save them?"

"Think about it." He spreads his hands. "It might not be as dramatic as the whole of humanity forgetting about the existence of the community, but it's an awfully big coincidence that right at the time the elves and dragons needed somewhere to flee to, Caolan met Alistair. I mean, Al doesn't even live in that part of the country, but Caolan just happened to go there, the exact right place, on the one day Alistair was there? A person who could take him directly to Percy, who was the *only* person who could grant sanctuary? That's one hell of a coincidence." He shrugs. "Or it was the magic lending a hand."

I run a hand through my hair. "I don't have the

details of what happened," I admit. "They haven't been widely shared. But yeah, that does sound a bit too perfect. So if we assume that the magic cares enough about us all to prevent us from being wiped out, then what's actually going on here? Because in a few thousand years, community species will be powerless. And for some of them, it's a short jump from there to extinction. How can vampires and incubi feed without their abilities?"

Noah's face tightens, probably because his boyfriend is a vampire and that hits home. Not that he'll have to worry about it—Andrew will be long dead before anything like that happens. "I don't know," he confesses. "There has to be something we're missing."

Drumming his fingers on the table, Fabian stares into space. "Not a weave, not a human spell," he muses. "Can we discard the idea that it's something someone did?"

"I suppose. But that brings us back to environmental factors." I sigh.

"How did you get onto the idea that it was a spell or weave anyway?" Noah asks, lifting his mug for another swallow of coffee. "It would be such a huge and complicated undertaking, for an outcome the instigator would never see."

"I know, but we were trying to think laterally. And if the species wars were the trigger, it's not that farfetched. Just impossible."

"The species wars," he muses. "The effects began to show within a few hundred years after, right?"

"We think. They were miniscule back then. If not for the correlation with the greater effects over time, you could call them statistical anomalies."

"And environmental is too farfetched as well, when you consider it had to be evenly distributed across two worlds in two different dimensions, not to mention the number of species." He puts his cup down with a *clink*. "I'm sorry. I wish I could have been more help, but I just don't see how it would work."

"Not your fault." I swallow down my disappointment. "Uh, I know you need to get to work, but before you go, is there any chance you could…" I gesture, a little embarrassed to even be asking.

He grins. It's not an expression I'm used to seeing on him, and it looks out of place. "You want a demonstration of my magic? Sure." His mug lifts from the table and glides across to the sink, where it hovers while the dishwasher door opens, and then the mug flips over and settles inside, perfectly positioned. I watch closely the whole time, but I can't see a single weave or anything else to indicate sorcery. It truly is a different type of power to what I have.

"Thank you. For tidying up, too," I add dryly. "Fabian likes to leave dishes in the sink." Noah stands, chuckling, and Fabian and I get up as well.

"I don't *like* to," Fabian protests. "I just get distracted by important things sometimes. I never leave them there too long."

It depends what you consider "too" long, but I don't say that, just smile affectionately at him and lift his hand to kiss it. The skin-warmed metal of his multiple rings brushes against my face. It's a sensation I never thought I'd come to love, but I do. It's quintessentially Fabian.

"You guys are so cute together, you make me wanna vomit," Noah declares, ruining the moment. But when I glance over, his smirk is friendly, despite the words. "I never would have thought Fabian would settle down."

Panic stabs my chest. *Shut the fuck up, Noah. Don't scare him off.* "That might be a stretch," I blurt. "We're just dating."

Noah frowns, and Fabian gasps, pulling his hand free and rounding on me. "We're what?"

Nervous butterflies take flight in my stomach. Was "dating" too strong a word? Should I have said we were just friends? "Uh—"

"Is that really what you think? That we're *dating*? How *could* you? I gave you one of my rings!"

His face is getting pink with emotion, his eyes are blazing, and the tips of his pointy ears are twitching, but I'm not entirely sure what's going on. Does this mean he thinks we're… serious?

Swallowing, I tamp down the happiness that wants to soar inside me. I might be getting my wires crossed. This is too important to fuck up—I'd rather have a little bit of Fabian than none at all.

"Fabian—" My voice is a croak, and I clear my throat. "I thought you wanted to just be casual. Friends who fuck. Remember?"

He stamps his foot. "That was *months* ago. Before we knew each other properly. Before we were spending all our free time together and I gave you one of my rings. What kind of idiot can't see that things are changing and he's in a relationship?" His indignation turns to sadness on those last words, and tears actually well up in his eyes. Noah reaches over and awkwardly pats his arm, looking like he wants to be anywhere but here.

Meanwhile, my heart is being ripped out of my chest. I've made Fabian cry.

"No," I manage. "No, I… I just didn't know… I thought you wanted to keep things casual, and I didn't want to scare you off. I'm an idiot," I confess. "I'm the world's biggest idiot. But all I want is for you to stay with me."

Fabian frowns and sniffles. "You thought I wanted us to be casual?"

"I really don't need to be here for this," Noah mutters, backing toward the door.

"Didn't you? You talked about us being friends."

"So, uh, I'll talk to you both later." Noah turns and flees. A moment later, I hear the front door open and shut and feel him passing through my wards.

"We *are* friends," Fabian protests. "We started that way. But then it became more. Like that movie."

I blink. "What movie?"

He waves me off. "I don't know what it's called. It was on cable one night."

"Well…" I choose my words carefully. "There's been a lot of discussion about your… um… lack of long-term relationships. And I thought that maybe you just weren't interested in being in one. I was happy to be whatever you wanted us to be."

"So you don't want us to be in a long-term relationship?"

"No! I mean, yes. I do want that. But only if you want it too. I don't want you to feel pressured or unhappy." Mustering my courage, I step closer and cup his cheek, brushing my thumb against his lips. Under my palm, the sharp bone structure of his face, once so alien, is now as familiar as the shape of my own. "I just want you however I can have you."

He draws in a breath, eyes on my face, then steps

back. Before my heart can shatter completely, he catches my hand and holds it up. "Do you see this?" He taps a finger against the ring I'm wearing. "This is a ring from my hoard."

I nod, clinging desperately to my hope.

"Dragons don't share their hoards randomly. We don't lend things that are in it. Some dragons don't even like to talk about what they hoard. I've known Steffen for thousands of years and have no idea what's in his hoard. A hoard is a very personal thing."

I nod again. "Okay."

"There are dragons who never give away anything from their hoards, not even to those they love most. For me to give you this ring, from my hoard, is a sign that you're not just a friend. We're not casual. We're not dating. You're my forever. I thought you knew this. I thought you accepted it. I thought…" He trails off, his breath catching, and I seize the moment, twisting my hand to capture his tightly and pull him close.

"Yes. I accept. Forever. I want that with you. I'm— I'm so honored to wear this. I was even before I knew what it meant, because it's yours. Please, I'm sorry I didn't understand. Don't be sad."

He makes a sound that might be a choked sob and buries his face against my neck. "I'm sorry. I should have made sure you knew what I wanted. I hate that all this time you've been so uncertain of me."

I hold him close, *my forever*, and savor the knowledge that I get to keep him. That this is what he wants too. "Let's just agree that we could have communicated better and stop being sorry. I don't want us to be swamped by regrets when we should be happy."

"Can I give you more rings?" he asks, voice muffled against my skin.

I grin. "Not one for every finger, but yes. I'd love to wear your rings."

He pulls back, then leans up to kiss me. "And you can buy me more."

This time, I laugh outright. "And I'll buy you more. As many as you want, and then more."

He sighs happily. "No wonder people like relationships. They get sex on tap, someone to indulge their dreams, and their best friend to snuggle with. It's winning all around." His smile turns wicked. "Let's go back to bed."

Yesss. "I can't," I say firmly, ignoring the part of me that thinks that's the best idea ever. "I need to get to work. But I'll skip lunch and come home early," I promise when Fabian pouts.

"Fiiiiine. I'll be waiting."

Nothing has ever sounded so good in my life.

CHAPTER FOURTEEN

Fabian

AFTER RHYS LEAVES FOR WORK, I clean up the kitchen—mostly to prove I can. He might be right that I leave things in the sink for longer than they should be there. If I lived alone, they might start growing mold before I remembered to deal with them. Now that I know how insecure he's been feeling about us, I'm determined to show him that I'm committed to him. To us.

Hmm, I might start by explaining that we're paired souls. I forgot to mention that before. And I'll give him another ring to wear. They look so good on his fingers, and that way I can see them more often. It's a shame he won't let me put a ring on every finger—multiple rings. And then he could lie back, naked, wearing my rings, and…

I shake off the fantasy. There's plenty of time for that later… when I convince Rhys to let me adorn him properly. For now, I need to think of ways to show him our eternal love is real. I might need some advice.

"Good morning, Fabian," Kethe says when I call her. "You're not tied to a tree somewhere, are you?"

Blinking, I look around me, just in case. No, I'm definitely in Rhys's living room. "Why would I be tied to a tree?"

"Why would you be tied anywhere? I've stopped asking myself how you come to be in certain situations. Although since you've been with Rhys, we've worried about you a lot less."

It hits me that she's referring to the times I hooked up with people and things got a bit carried away. But that hasn't happened in a long time. I have Rhys now.

"I'm not tied up," I assure her, even as I mentally note that Rhys and I haven't done that for a while. I didn't think he'd be into it, since he was so repressed before, but I was wrong. He's astonishingly keen to both be tied up and to tie me up. We've had a lot of fun with it. "I do need your help, though."

"What's wrong? Is Rhys okay?" I hear a clank in the background, then footsteps. "Okay, I'm sitting down. You have my full attention. Tell me what you need."

I love Kethe.

"Rhys needs to know how much I love him," I declare, then launch into a recap of what happened this morning.

"He didn't know you'd committed to him?" Kethe sounds shocked. "But… did he think you just tell everyone you're with that you love them?"

I hesitate. "I'm supposed to actually say the words?"

"Fabian!"

That would be a yes. "How was I supposed to know that? I've never done this whole love thing before. I stopped having sex with other people and gave him one of my rings. Shouldn't he have known what that means?"

She sighs, a long, "why is this my life" kind of sigh. "He's not a mind reader, Fabian. He probably knew you cared about him, but not how far it goes. Have you still not said you love him? Not even this morning?"

"I told him he's my forever," I defend myself. "That counts, right?" Why is this so hard? It's never so hard in the movies.

Although, come to think, in the movies they *do* say "I love you."

"It's a start," Kethe mutters. "If you really want him to feel secure, you need to tell him you love him. Rhys isn't like you, Fabian. You literally don't care what anyone else thinks of you. You're confident to extremes most people don't have. And you're comfortable in any environment, with any people. You have no doubt that Rhys loves you, because you see the things he does for you and accept what they mean. But Rhys sees what you do for him, and I'll bet he knows they mean you care but then second-guesses how far that goes. He questions all the little details. He needs the words, straight out, no hedging."

This is worse than I thought. "You think he really doesn't know how I feel?"

"Even if he does, would it hurt to say the words?"

Good point. "It needs to be special," I decide. "What can I do to make it special?"

"Think about what's important to Rhys," Kethe begins, but I've had an idea.

"We could go to that rooftop restaurant, and I'll have them spell out his name and the words 'I Love You' in fireworks!"

"Is that even possible?" she asks doubtfully. "I don't think fireworks work that way."

I frown. Maybe not. I don't know enough about fire-works to be sure. "I'll call you back, Kethe. I need to do some research on fireworks."

"No! If you start researching, you'll forget everything else. Nothing that needs research."

Hmm. She might be right. "Okay, no fireworks. What about a flash mob? That would be lots of fun, and what says 'I love you' more than a group of people singing a love song?"

"A group of strangers, you mean? In a public place? Where all eyes would be on you?"

I feel like she's hinting at something, but I'm not sure what. "Yes?"

"Fabian, do you really think Rhys would enjoy being the center of attention like that?"

I think about my Rhys, how he gets pink if more than a few people are listening to him talk, the way he crowds close to me when there are a lot of people around, and how he told me once that he loves his lab because it's just him and his work, nobody watching, nobody judging, and realize what she means.

"Dinner at home. And maybe we can watch a few episodes of that show he hates but still watches because of some of the characters."

Kethe's sigh this time is relieved. "That sounds perfect."

"I'll cook!"

"That does not sound perfect. Fabian—"

"I won't try to do anything fancy," I assure her, although Rhys does love cheese soufflé. It can't be *that* hard to make, can it? "And I'll follow a recipe."

"What if you get distracted?" she demands. "Do you

really think Rhys wants to come home to find his house burned down?"

It was definitely the right decision to call Kethe. She thinks of all the important details.

"What if I prepare the food using my magic?" I suggest. I've never done that before, but the magic-person character on the show we might watch tonight does it, so it's probably possible. Although that is a human show with made-up magic. "Can that be done?"

"Yes," she says reluctantly. "You need to know what the food is supposed to look like and taste like, though."

"Easy!"

"And you need to be focused while you're doing it. No thinking of other things. You wouldn't want Rhys to choke because you were thinking of rings while you were 'cooking' and one ended up in the middle of the food."

"That would be bad," I agree. "Although it would be interesting to see what kind of ring I ended up with."

Silence.

"I'm kidding," I assure her. "I promise, I'll concentrate. And if anything seems off, I'll order takeout."

"I guess I can't ask more than that. Call me for help if you run into trouble," she adds.

"I will. Promise." I start to pull the phone away from my ear.

"And Fabian?"

Putting the phone back, I say, "Yeah?"

"Congratulations. I'm so happy for you."

The grin takes me by surprise and stretches my mouth so wide, my cheeks hurt. "Me too."

Turns out, planning a romantic evening at home takes a lot more effort than a flash mob or sky-writing fireworks would. It's not just enough to have food. I go through most of Rhys's cupboards and drawers before deciding we need a special tablecloth and napkins to set the scene. The nearest department store doesn't have what I want, and I don't have time to run all over town looking, so I use my magic to create one.

Then I have to think carefully about which episodes of the show we should watch. There's a lot of killing and some heartbreak, so I don't want to risk Rhys picking an episode that will ruin the mood. It's a conundrum, but fortunately, YouTube has the answer in the form of a forty-minute edit of romantic moments between Rhys's two favorite characters. I add it to my favorites so I can find it easily later.

Next… dinner. Since I'm not actually cooking it, I decide to go with something fancy after all. Keeping in mind what Kethe said about me needing to know how it should taste, I surf some foodie sites looking for inspiration. Something I've eaten before that's delicious and posh *and* that Rhys likes. It's too hard to choose, so I end up conjuring samples of a few different dishes and taste-testing them. I'll ask what he's in the mood for when he gets home and then impress him by preparing it on the spot!

Which leaves ambiance. I might not be an expert on romantic relationships, but I watch a lot of TV and movies. I know what romance looks like. We need candles, lots of them, clustered on every surface, which means another trip to the store. Damn, I should have thought about this earlier.

Back at the store, I head straight to the candle

department. They have a good range, but not as many as I think I'll need. I'm counting on my fingers when one of the store employees hesitates beside me with a suggestive smile.

"Can I do something for you?"

It's far from the first time in my life that I've been flirted with, so I know the signs. I'm about to flirt back— because flirting doesn't have to go anywhere, and it's fun —but I'm not sure how Rhys feels about stuff like that, and I'm in a committed relationship now. I care about his feelings and don't want to do anything that would make him feel bad.

So instead, I just smile politely. "Do you have any more candles?"

The cute young thing glances at the shelves in front of me in confusion. There are dozens of candles in different shapes and sizes there. "Uh… how many do you need?"

I shrug. "I'm not sure, exactly? Maybe a hundred? Maybe more. But if I use any of these scented ones, they have to be all the same scent, because mixing the scents might give us headaches, right?"

He blinks at me. "Uh… I guess? But if you're lighting them all at the same time, you don't want them all to be scented anyway. It would be kind of strong. Unless it's a really big room? Or outside."

Shaking my head, I turn back to studying the shelf. "That's a good point. The room's a good size, but not huge."

Cutie—whose name tag says Ryder—frowns at the candles. "What are you using them for? There are some in the back, but not a lot."

I hold up my hands like I'm framing a picture. "It's

going to be an unforgettable night of romance. I'm telling my boyfriend that I love him." It's the first time I've used the word "boyfriend" in relation to myself, and it gives me shivers. Good ones.

Ryder's face lights up. "Seriously? Oh my god, that's so epic. Catrina!" he calls to another employee passing by, a middle-aged woman. "This customer—" He glances at me inquiringly.

"Fabian," I supply.

"Fabian is going to tell his boyfriend he loves him and he wants to fill the room with candles."

Catrina presses her hands to her chest and sighs. "Really? That's amazing. I wish someone would do that for me." She looks me up and down. "Your boyfriend is so lucky."

"I'm the lucky one. He makes every moment seem like the best one of my life."

"Awww," they say in unison.

"So you want to fill the room with candles?" Catrina asks. "Like when Monica proposed to Chandler on *Friends*?"

"Yes!" She gets it. "Exactly like that."

"Like what?" Ryder's confusion is adorable. Catrina narrows her eyes.

"Don't say a single word that might remind me you're too young to have watched *Friends*."

"I'm not," he protests. "I mean, they play repeats sometimes on cable. And my mom loves it."

"Oh my god, his *mom*," she mutters.

"Um, can we focus, please? I'm running out of time," I say, drawing their attention back to me. "If it helps, I've seen *Friends*. And loved it." I don't mention that I'm old enough to have been grandparent to ancestors they don't even know they have. I look like a twenty-year-old, and that's good enough.

"Thank you," she says, smiling at me. "Okay, candles. I don't want to rain on your parade, but while it's a super romantic idea, that many candles is going to be hot and messy and maybe a fire hazard."

My heart sinks.

"But…" She holds up a finger. "…there are these really cool battery-operated candles in the party department. You could mix them up, have some real ones nearest to you, then the rest with batteries. That way you don't need to keep an eye on them all."

Hmm. "Do they look fake? Because I need this to be special, not plastic."

She beckons. "Come and see."

We head toward the party department. The store is pretty quiet, and Ryder calls out to someone else about what we're doing. Some of the customers overhear, and by the time we get to a display of battery-operated candles in pretty jars, we have a small entourage.

"…and then he said his boyfriend makes every moment feel like the best one ever," Ryder concludes, and there's a chorus of oooohhhhs.

"Is he good-looking? Your boyfriend," a grandmotherly woman asks me, and I obligingly pull out my phone.

"He's beautiful." I turn the phone to show them a photo I took of Rhys while he was working, with that cute crease he gets between his eyebrows when he concentrates.

"Very hot nerd," a woman with an infant strapped to her chest says approvingly. "He looks all intense too."

"He is," I agree.

"And you guys are monogamous? Not looking for a

third or anything?" a hipster-looking guy with a mustache grooming kit in his basket asks. The rest of the group turns to stare at him. "What?" he says defensively. "It can't hurt to ask."

"Fabian's about to declare his *love*." Ryder plants his hands on his hips.

"That doesn't mean they don't want to share that love," the hipster returns. "You don't know what they like."

"Not sharing," I say firmly. "But thanks for the offer. Now, candles?"

We turn our attention to the display. They look much better than I imagined they would, even the ones that aren't in jars. They're designed to appear partly burned down, so the "wicks" are inside the candle, giving a nice glowy effect.

"How many of these do you have?" I ask, mentally planning where to put real candles and where these ones could go. Catrina goes to check inventory.

"Fabian, dear," the grandmotherly woman says, "have you planned what you're going to wear? Is it ironed?"

I look down at my clothes. "I can't just wear this?" They're clean and mostly neat. A few wrinkles, but I don't need to iron them to fix that. Magic will do it in a fraction of the time.

"No, you cannot," she declares. "Let's go to menswear."

"I have other clothes," I protest as she grabs my arm above the elbow and tows me along.

"I'm sure you do. But I can't inspect them, so you'll just have to buy some more."

It takes another fifteen minutes for her—with help

from the rest of the entourage—to pick my outfit, make me try it on, and deem it acceptable. These humans are awfully bossy. Maybe that's their hidden ability now that they no longer use magic.

Something stirs in the back of my brain, and I stop arguing with Mirna (the grandmother) and try to remember whatever it is that's bothering me. It has to do with humans using magic…

Fingers snap in front of my eyes. "Fabian, concentrate! You don't have time to daydream."

I blink. She's right. "I need to buy a ring."

The group gasps in unison. It's very impressive.

"Are you going to *propose?*" Keilie breathes. Her baby, Morgan, is teething and only sleeps when she walks him around, and she's been in the store for hours.

"Might be a bit soon for that," hipster Deakin offers.

As one, the others glare at him.

"What? He hasn't even said he loves him yet. That needs to come first."

"He's right," Ryder concedes sadly. "He needs to be secure in your love before you can propose."

"I'm not planning to propose. I just want to buy a ring. Maybe more than one." I hold up my beringed hands. "I like rings."

Mirna purses her lips. "Is this really the time for frivolous shopping? You have more important things to think about."

"Buying rings for Rhys is important. He knows how much I like them and that me buying some for him has meaning." At least, he does after our discussion this morning. Maybe even before that, since he doesn't take off the one I gave him even to sleep. "Do you have rings here?"

Ryder and Catrina exchange glances. "Well, yeah. Did you want fancy ones, though? Because there's not many of those. Most are just junk jewelry. And there's really not many options for men."

"Even junk can be pretty," I proclaim loftily. I really don't care what my rings are made of, although I have to be more careful with the cheap ones, since they don't last as long.

So we all trek over to the jewelry department. Catrina's right, there aren't a lot of options "for men"—don't even get me started on the gross stupidity of classing jewelry by gender instead of style—but there's a decent range of women's sizes, so I just pick what I like in the size to fit my and Rhys's fingers. They have some pretty things, some with intricate filigree work, some plain with simple stones, a few really cool chunky designs. I settle on four fairly quickly.

When I eventually leave the store, pushing a cart filled with different kinds of candles, batteries to go in some of them, a new outfit and accessories, and a plush bear that says "I Love You"—Deakin's addition, in case I fuck things up—I'm surrounded by my entourage. They help me load the car, dispensing advice the whole time, then create a WhatsApp chat for us all so I can let them know how the night goes. I think I've been adopted by a posse of humans, and I'm scared of what Percy and Brandt—and Steffen—are going to say when they find out. Steffen may confiscate my phone and lock me in my room forever.

Whatever. I like humans. They're so cluelessly interesting, thinking that their gods are real and that they have no magic.

Back at Rhys's place—dare I say our place?—I whiz

through the remaining preparations, and when I'm done, the place looks amazing. I take a quick shower, put on my new clothes, and wait for him to come home.

After five minutes, I'm deathly bored. I'm making a conscious effort not to start working or even think about something that could distract me, because I want to be aware when Rhys gets here and lavish all my attention on him. But I need to do something or my brain will explode with boredom.

So I pull out my phone and google "can fireworks spell out words." Kethe said no, but she might be wrong. She's not a fireworks expert, after all. And even though I agree with her that a quiet night in is a much better option for this special date, I might want to send Rhys a fireworks message sometime in the future.

But it seems Kethe was mostly right. While you technically can spell out words one letter at a time, the kind of epic cursive love message I was envisioning isn't yet possible. However, a comment on one site leads me down an unexpected path to the concept of drones.

Light-up drones.

It would be like a message written by a firefly!

I could have a *swarm* of them, spelling out a whole *poem* of love. Maybe some of them could scatter glitter too. There's something so special about glitter. Nothing says love more than finding tiny sparkles in your underwear three days later. After all, what's love if not tiny sparkles attached to your body?

Or something. I still haven't learned all the ins and outs of this relationship thing.

I hear the garage door opening and put my phone away. When Rhys comes in, looking tired but happy, he's greeted by an armful of smiling me.

"Hi," he says, clearly delighted. "This is nice."

"You're important to me," I declare, and his smile softens.

"Thank you, Fabian. You're important to me too." He kisses me, a gentle, warm kind of kiss that's not leading to sex. I never had many of these kisses before Rhys, but now I crave them. Just being with someone and wanting to kiss them, be near them… it's special.

When our lips finally part, I turn my face into his neck and breathe deeply of his scent. He's so warm and comfortable there. It's my special spot to just bask in his presence.

"Hey," he murmurs. "Think we can get out of the hallway?"

I laugh and pry myself from his arms. "I guess so. I have special plans for us. You should go shower and change."

"Are we going out?" He sounds a bit disappointed, and I mentally thank Kethe for being the voice of reason.

"Nope! Special plans just for us, here at home."

His smile comes back, blindingly bright, just a little bit shy, but definitely happy that he gets to spend the evening with me, and I kick myself for ever letting him feel even a second of insecurity. My science nerd needs lots of petting and reassurance, and I'm going to make sure he gets it every day.

Starting now.

"Before you go, I bought you something today. Well, two somethings." I reach into my pocket and pull out the rings I got for him. Two of the four are already on my hand, but these two I picked just for him. "You don't have to wear them all at once," I add, remembering that he was hesitant to have a ring on every finger. "And if you don't like them, I'll find others to give you."

He looks at the rings I lay in his palm, and his smile gets even wider. "Thank you, Fabian. They're lovely." His glance is sly. "You really do want to adorn me with rings, don't you?"

"Yes," I admit. "The thought of you wearing my hoard is sexier than anything else ever in the history of time."

His kiss this time takes me by surprise, and it's a whole lot hotter than the last one. We eventually break apart to breathe, both mussed and sweaty and panting, and Rhys leans in to whisper, "I love the thought of being your personal ring model."

Then he backs away. "I'm going to shower. Looking forward to your plans."

…plans?

☙

"WELL." Rhys lays his napkin on the table and beams at me. "Dinner was superb, Fabian. You have a gift for planning the perfect date."

I smile back, feeling smug. Dinner *was* good. Conjuring food is such a breeze. I don't know why people complain about cooking. "It's only just beginning," I promise. "Sit there and finish your wine while I get everything ready."

He looks intrigued. "I could get a start on washing up," he offers, but I shake my head.

"I promise I'll take care of the dishes before bed, but you're not washing up. This is supposed to be a romantic evening. Dishes aren't romantic."

Leaning over to kiss my cheek, he says, "Everything is romantic when I do it with you."

I snort and quirk an eyebrow. "Really?"

"Well, no." He laughs. "But it seemed like the right thing to say on our romantic date."

I hand him his half-empty wineglass and then retreat to the living room. He hasn't been in here since he got home, which is just as well, since candles are everywhere. It takes me nearly fifteen minutes to either turn on or light them all. I could use magic, but that feels like cheating. Isn't part of the romance the effort involved? I had to magic dinner or risk maybe accidentally poisoning Rhys with my cooking, but this is something that's well within my capabilities.

But I'm about ninety-nine percent sure that Rhys is taking advantage of my absence to wash the dishes. I have excellent hearing, and drinking wine doesn't make that sloshing sound. I could scold him, but if this makes him happy, why should I ruin it for him?

That doesn't stop me from giving him a reproachful look and shaking my head when I go back into the kitchen. He smiles sheepishly as he slots the last plate into the drying rack. "Sorry?"

"No you're not. But it's done now. Come on, it's time to cuddle on the couch and watch TV."

"You have the best ideas." He obediently follows me into the living room, then stops dead and gasps. I smirk. The room looks awesome. It's aglow with all the candles, a warm, inviting den of romance.

"Oh wow, Fabian." He lifts his hand to cover his mouth briefly. "How did you do this?"

"I had some help," I admit. I've been ignoring the vibration of my phone in my pocket for over an hour, pretty sure it's just messages from my human posse asking how tonight's going. And maybe some from Kethe. If there was an emergency, people would be calling Rhys's phone as well.

"It's amazing." He slides his arms around me and squeezes. "I'm the luckiest person alive."

I want to say something about how *I'm* actually the lucky one, but the words are stuck behind the lump in my throat. Because he really believes that… that being with me makes him lucky. Kethe was right when she said I've never had self-esteem issues, never questioned my place and value, but I've still never felt as wanted and loved as I do right now, knowing that Rhys considers himself lucky to have me in his life.

This whole love thing is better than any drug I ever took, even those weird swamp weeds when I was still a fledgling that made me hiccup tiny flowers for two days.

"Me too," I finally manage. "C'mon." I lead him to the couch and settle in with his warmth beside me. In the soft light of the candles, his skin is luminous, but not as much as his expression. This was the best thing I could have done to show him my feelings.

I dig out my phone and cast the saved video to the TV.

"What's…" He trails off, his mouth falling open. "We're watching a Malec edit?"

"Forty minutes of the most romantic moments," I confirm. "I need tips so I can continue to impress you with my dating finesse."

He laughs but grabs my hand and laces our fingers together. Looks like I picked another winner.

I'm not lying about the tips, though. Rhys thinks this show is only okay, but he still re-watches episodes occasionally just for these two characters. It's gotta be like a secret scrapbook, right?

Sure enough, it's only a few moments before he's smiling and sighing, and I have to admit, I can see the appeal. Both actors are extremely hot, and there's a mix of steamy kisses and tender moments, intense sexual tension and laughing companionship.

Then we get to a breakup scene, and I sit bolt upright. "What? No! It's supposed to be romantic! YouTube is ruining our date night!"

"I don't think this is YouTube's fault," Rhys murmurs, not taking his eyes off the screen. "And it *is* romantic. He's breaking up with him because it's the only way to give him back his magic and make him feel whole."

I turn to stare at my boyfriend's profile. "What?"

Rhys sighs, grabs the remote and hits pause, then turns to face me. "What, what?"

"Explain why they're breaking up."

"Maybe we should watch the whole series together," Rhys muses. "We could skip a lot of the boring scenes."

"I doubt it would be quicker than you just explaining it to me right now." I'm not used to being the patient, logical one in this relationship, but he can't seriously think watching the whole series is the answer here.

"Probably not," he concedes. "Okay, so Magnus— that guy"—he points at the screen—"is a warlock who has magic. Except he gave it up to his father to help save Alec's friend. Alec is his boyfriend, that guy there," he adds helpfully. "His father is a demon—not our kind, the human hell kind."

"That was very noble and self-sacrificing of him, though from the way you said he doesn't feel whole, I bet he regrets it. How is breaking up going to get his magic back?"

"Alec went to Magnus's father and made a bargain: Magnus gets his magic back if they break up."

I think about it. "That's a pretty dumb bargain," I point out. "I'm guessing the hell demon doesn't approve of their relationship?"

Rhys shakes his head. "He wants to manipulate Magnus and thinks it'll be easier if he's brokenhearted and Alec's not around."

"Smart. Not that I approve of his actions, but all my knowledge of past wars spells out pretty clearly that the best way to win is to isolate your enemy and strike when they're weakened."

He gives me a weird look. "That's... not what you're supposed to be getting from this."

Oh. I try again. "The hell demon should be ashamed of himself. I hope Angus and Mac find a way to get back together and keep the magic." There. I smile smugly.

"Magnus and Alec," he corrects.

Oops.

"And they do," he continues. "But then some other stuff—you know what, we should just keep watching." He picks up the remote but hesitates, his gaze on me.

"What?"

"Would you feel less than whole if you lost your magic?"

The question stuns me like a blow. I'm not sure why —we were just talking about the subject. It's a reasonable extension of the conversation. But it still takes my breath away.

"Yes." It sounds raw, and I swallow. "Especially because my ability to change forms is tied to my magic. Without it, I'd be forever trapped in only one form." I shudder at the thought. Trapped in my biped body, I would forever lose my natural form. My ability to fly. But if I were trapped in dragon form, I would lose everything my biped shape gives me, beginning with the non-dragons I've come to hold so dear. We dragons are no longer beings of one shape—my very soul is tied to being both dragon and biped. To be only one would make me unbalanced—

Fuck. Me.

I sit up sharply.

"Fabian?" Rhys sounds startled.

"I need the archive," I say abruptly.

"Ah… okay."

No, wait… tonight is about Rhys and me. This can wait. If I'm right, one night will make no difference. And if I'm wrong, then it really doesn't matter at all.

Resolutely, I push the whole idea to the back of my brain and settle back on the couch, smiling at my beautiful, bewildered boyfriend. "I'll do it tomorrow. Tonight is our night."

His answering smile is a little confused but happy, and he lifts the remote and hits Play, then snuggles up beside me.

The scene resumes on the screen, and I force myself to focus on the moment and not start thinking about magic and losing it and what impact that might have on more than just the person who loses it. The next clip is of them kissing, so presumably things got better, but then they're apart again? And the tall one whose name isn't Mac is crying.

This show is an emotional roller coaster, and I'm just watching bits of it.

It finally finishes on a wedding, with everyone smiling and looking blissful, and Rhys sighs contentedly. "That was great. Thanks for indulging me."

This is my opening, and I'm suddenly nervous. It's ridiculous. I'm absolutely secure in the knowledge that Rhys loves me back and that we're going to be together forever. But still my hands want to shake as I gather myself to speak.

"Indulging you is what I want to do for the rest of our lives together," I say. "I love you."

His jaw drops, then he lunges forward and kisses me so hard, our teeth clatter together. I don't care. This is the perfect reaction.

When he pulls back, he's grinning widely. "I love you too. So much. And this…" He looks around the room. "All this is amazing, but all I need is you."

"You've got me," I promise. "How do you feel about having your name written in the sky with fireworks?"

CHAPTER FIFTEEN

Rhys

WHEN I WAKE on Saturday morning after a night of romance and very energetic sex, I'm smiling. In fact, I'm pretty sure it's the same smile that was on my face when I fell asleep, the one that followed me into my wonderful dreams of Fabian as a Shadowhunter. Spoiler: he wasn't very good at it, but he looked delicious. And he still managed to somehow rescue me from the various beasties that had captured me.

It seems I might have a rescue fantasy.

Chuckling a little, I prop myself up and glance around the room. Fabian's side of the bed is empty, and he's not here, which means he's probably working downstairs. It didn't escape me that something occurred to him last night, and he's probably been desperate to dig into whatever it was. But he stayed with me instead.

Why yes, I *am* feeling delightfully smug today. I'm loved by an amazing, sexy dragon who pulled out all the stops to show me what I mean to him, even ignoring the other great love of his life: his work.

Sighing, I stretch, then roll to the edge of the bed

and get up. Fabian might be working now, but we have plans to go to Here Be Dragons this afternoon so he can get in a flight, then we'll have dinner with his family and spend the night. It's become routine for us to spend at least a few hours every weekend with his family, and not just because Fabian needs to shift regularly. If it was just that, he could do it during the week while I'm working—it's not like his job is locked into business hours.

No, the reason we spend so much time at Here Be Dragons is that it feels like home. I love Fabian's family —even Steffen—and they seem to like me too. Now that I know for sure that Fabian doesn't consider me a convenient friend to fuck, the shackles of insecurity have fallen away, and I can see that I'm not just "that nice guy with Fabian" to them.

I head into the bathroom to use the facilities and have a quick shower, and when I come back out, wrapped in a towel, my phone is ringing. It's Sura, and I only hesitate for a second before answering. She had to listen to me babble out the whole story of Fabian's and my miscommunication yesterday, and then spent an hour lecturing me because I hadn't told Fabian what my relationship expectations were. She deserves to know how it all turned out.

"Hey," I greet her.

"Don't hey me. You were supposed to call or message last night after you talked to Fabian. I waited up!"

"You did not. You were probably up anyway. Or out," I add. I'm pretty sure she mentioned something about a party.

"That's not the point," she dodges, which means I'm

right. "The point is that you were supposed to let me know how it went."

"I never had to say anything. Fabian was waiting with a fabulous dinner, a gift that shows me how much I mean to him, the most romantic half hour of television that ever existed, and then he said he loved me. I think he's clear on what I need from our relationship."

Silence.

"Wow," she says eventually. "That goes to show just how well he knows you. And proves my point that this is all your fault. He didn't know you were unhappy because you didn't tell him."

"I was never unhappy," I deny, standing and using a simple sorcery weave to fetch some clothes from the walk-in. "I was insecure." I switch the phone to speaker, set it on the bed, and begin to dress. Sura's probably going to lecture for a while, and since Fabian's not here, there's no point in staying naked.

No sooner do I think it than I hear the clatter of footsteps running through the house.

"Rhys!" Fabian bursts in just as I pull my T-shirt over my head. "Come and see this." He grabs my hand.

"Good morning, Fabian," Sura says dryly from the phone.

Fabian casts it a distracted glance. "Hi, Sura. He'll call you back. This is important." His face is creased with a frown, but his eyes are alight. This is something big.

"I'll talk to you later, Sura," I say slowly, grabbing the phone. What could it be about? The thing he thought of last night?

"Yeah, whatever. Bye." She's laughing as the call disconnects.

I let Fabian pull me out of the bedroom and down to the kitchen, where his laptop and a notebook are spread on the table amid a messy pile of papers.

"I used your printer this morning," he says, noticing where my eye has fallen.

"That's fine. I've told you that. But what is this?" The script on the pages is unreadable to me, probably in his native language—or an extinct language, for all I know.

"I think I've got the answer, Rhys. To why your abilities are fading."

The bottom falls out of my world, and I stumble into a chair, gripping it hard and then deciding to just sit in it. "Really?" I croak.

He shrugs. "I think so. I can't be sure without asking Brandt to check with the life force. But it all makes sense."

"Is it… Can we fix it?"

This time he hesitates. "Theoretically, yes. But the solution might be worse than the problem. It depends on your perspective."

Okay, this sounds fucked-up.

"Walk me through it," I say, trying to sound calm and not like I want to vomit. "And then I guess we need to call everyone else working on the project. And Brandt or… someone." Brandt, the lucifer, and the elf king can all communicate with the existential magic—as much as it communicates with anyone. If Fabian's theory is correct, they'll be able to confirm it and tell us if our solutions will work. I'm not sure exactly how it works, but from what I've heard, it was a big factor in whatever happened around the time the elves and dragons migrated to Earth.

Someone has to fill me in on that backstory one day. As soon as we've resolved this.

"It's been bugging me for months," he says, sliding into the chair beside mine and turning his laptop to face us. "Something about humans. Something I heard or read but couldn't remember. But then last night, Angus and Mac reminded me."

I bite my lip to keep from correcting him. It's not important, and I don't want him to get off track. Even if it is beyond belief that anyone could forget Malec's names.

"How so?" I ask instead.

"When Angus lost his magic, he wasn't whole. And if that happened to me, I wouldn't be whole, but it would also impact the people around me. I'd no longer be able to shift forms. Our relationship would change, at the very least, if not be destroyed. My family would be impacted. My job. If all dragons lost their magic, the very world would be impacted. Things would need to change in order to accommodate how we'd changed."

"Okay," I say slowly.

"We've talked before about this being environmental. Something that changed across two dimensions that affected all species."

I shake my head. "But we ruled that out. There's nothing that could have changed so evenly across both dimensions that would affect every species."

"There *is*. The life force itself."

It feels as though all the oxygen in the room is sucked away.

"The magic?" I gasp. "You think there's a problem with the existential magic that makes up everything?" Oh no. Fuck. Oh fuck no. "Are we... Do you think we're heading toward…" I can't finish the sentence. The thought of an apocalypse or worse, the end of everything, is just too much to process without coffee.

I need coffee.

"Is there coffee?" I ask, cutting off whatever Fabian was about to tell me. He blinks, mouth open, then points to the counter. I stumble out of my chair and fix myself a cup, then return to him, sipping the brain-clearing elixir. "Okay. Sorry. You were going to tell me the end of the world is nigh." I gulp my coffee.

The sound he makes might be a chuckle. "No, I wasn't. The world's just fine. There's no *problem* with the life force, exactly."

Carefully, I set my mug down on the table. The *clink* it makes is a little firmer than I intended, but fortunately, nothing sloshes over the side. "Fabian, explain this faster and with a lot less drama, please. I don't think I can take the suspense."

He looks almost wounded. "I'm not dramatic. But fine. Think about it. We've had all the pieces in front of us this whole time, but just never put it together."

"Fabian!"

"What happened right before the decline in abilities began?"

I glare at him, but he just waits for me to reply. "The species wars."

"What, more specifically?"

I draw a blank. "The near annihilation of the community?"

"By…?"

I'm going to strangle him.

"By humans," I snap, and it hits me. "Fuck, the humans. They lost their memories of us. But how would that…?" The rest of it sinks in. Knowledge I only gained recently. "Their ability to use magic."

"Exactly." Fabian shakes his head. "I don't know how we missed it."

"Walk me through what you're thinking." I'm still not sure I can get my head around it.

"It's about balance. The life force balances everything in existence. We don't always see that because the other side of the coin might not be happening *here*. The life force has everything and everywhere to work with… so we might take an action, but the resulting balance happens elsewhere."

"Sure. Like the butterfly effect."

He stares at me blankly. "What?"

I wave a hand. "Never mind. So you think the result of humans not using their inborn ability is that the rest of us also lose our abilities? To balance things out?" I think I'm going to hyperventilate.

Fabian's expression changes from excited to alarmed. "Rhys, you need to calm down. Take a deep breath." He grabs my hand and places it on his chest. "Breathe in time with me."

Just his touch makes me feel calmer, but I obediently begin drawing in deep breaths in time with him, pushing the thought of losing my abilities as some form of cosmic balance out of my head.

Finally, Fabian smiles and leans forward to kiss me. "There we go. It's going to be okay."

I slump back in my chair but keep hold of his hand. "How can it be? You said yourself that losing your magic would break you. You wouldn't be whole. It's the same for me." I blink away tears. "Is it likely the process will speed up? I know right now it doesn't look like total loss of ability will happen in my lifetime, but why is it happening so slowly?"

Fabian squeezes my hand. "Because the life force is giving us the chance to fix things."

"...so this gradual decrease is because the magic is on our side and wants us to stop it?" Imani asks, sounding as confused as I am. Fabian and I made some frantic calls and managed to get everyone to the DEA offices within a couple of hours, and now we're facing a bunch of people who aren't thrilled about being called in to work on a Saturday just to be told the answer to the problem that's been bugging us is that we're being forced to pay the price for another species' transgression.

"Yes," Fabian says to the packed room. The project team is here, plus the elf king and some of his senior advisors, the lucifer and his senior team, and Brandt, Percy, Sophie, and Steffen... who's visibly jumpy about having so many people crammed in with Brandt. "I believe so. I can't think of any other reason for it. The life force requires balance, but it knows the toll this would take, both psychologically and in a practical sense, so this gradual decrease both allows us time to rectify the issue *and*, in the event we can't, will mean the smallest impact possible on the world. It will just be that your abilities slowly dwindle until you can barely use them at all, while you evolve ways to compensate, and then one day, a generation is born without them." He spreads his hands. "They can't miss what they never knew."

I don't need to look around the room to know how everyone's reacting to that.

"But if this is a result of what humans did here on Earth, why is it affecting us also?" Caolan asks. "Until recently, we were all but completely separate from Earth, dating back to before…" He gropes for the right word. "…the event."

"The event?" Alistair Smythe, a hellhound working for the lucifer, snickers.

"Shut up, Alistair," several people chorus in unison.

I don't even want to know.

"But our dimensions are—were—linked," Fabian explains. "In all our history, we've never been able to safely travel to any other dimension but this one." He looks at the older elf sitting beside the king. "Or at least, that's what dragon records show. Eerika?"

She nods. "Elf records are the same. There have been portals opened to other dimensions, but either they were inhospitable to the point we were unable to even cross through, or the elves who did enter never returned. Earth is the only place we were able to visit safely."

"And we did so regularly right up until the species wars began," the king says sadly, looking at Brandt. "Are we included in this because of our hubris? Could we have done something to turn the humans from their course?"

Brandt sighs. "I don't know. Maybe we were too quick to withdraw and abandon the community to the humans."

"Let's not start laying blame," the lucifer says quietly, and I take the chance to study him. He's only been in the job a few years, and he's younger than any other lucifer I've ever heard of—like, human young. I think in his forties? It's almost frightening to think the governance of the whole world is in his hands.

But he does have the magic on his side. The magic that's slowly stripping us of everything that makes us who we are.

I push down the nausea and tune back in.

"…now that we understand what happened, we need to think about the next steps," Lucifer Sam is saying. "You're right, Fabian. Your theory is correct. The magic confirms it."

Fabian glances to Brandt, almost involuntarily, and Brandt nods. So does the king.

"Wow. Okay, that's… well, it's not good. But at least we know what we're dealing with now."

I've never before heard Fabian so uncertain. But then he takes a breath, and his confidence returns.

"This next bit I'm not quite as sure about," he says, sounding anything but unsure. "It's my hope that the life force will confirm it, or at least let us know if we're on the right track."

"Your plan to fix it, you mean?" Imani asks. She looks a bit shellshocked but not as much as some of the others in the room.

"Yes. I believe that to stop, and maybe even reverse what's been done, we need to restore the balance."

There's a long moment of confused silence. Fabian didn't tell me this bit, so I'm in the same boat as everyo—

"Absolutely fucking not!" Gideon Bailey roars, making most of us flinch. He lurches to his feet, eyes blazing. "I'll allow this to happen over my dead body!"

What… oh.

Oh *fuck* no.

I turn on Fabian. "You want to remind humans how to use magic?" I hiss. "Tell them about us? Are you *mad?*"

A rumble goes around the room. The elves and dragons are quiet, mostly staying out of it, but the rest of us… well, we've spent nine thousand years hiding from humans because they tried to wipe us out. And frankly, not a lot of what we see them doing to each other makes us think they wouldn't try again if they knew about us.

Fabian holds up his hands. "This is not my decision to make," he says soothingly. "I'm merely pointing out an option."

"The only option, I'm afraid," the lucifer says, the words sounding like they're dragged from him. Heads turn toward him, mouths dropping open in shock. "Sit down, Gideon," he tells his boyfriend. "The magic confirms that the only way to stop the deterioration is to restore balance… by having humans relearn to use magic."

"Fuck," Noah, the only human in the room, says sharply. "Fuck fuck fuck. This is *not* a good idea, Sam."

The lucifer shrugs helplessly. "It's that or watch our abilities slowly fade away. I-I can't bear the thought of shifter children never learning how to shift."

There's a chorus of sounds from the shifters in the room that make my heart want to break.

"I can't believe it," Imani says, tears beginning to trickle down her face. "They'll kill us. How is this balance? They'll wipe us out, and there will be no balance."

I can't breathe. She's right, and my chest hurts, and I can't breathe. Whatever we do, we're dooming our descendants. They either die in war and strife with humans or slowly dwindle to being all but human themselves. Worse… I look over at Andrew Turner, a vampire who's rumored to have witnessed the signing of the Magna Carta. Without their abilities, species like vampires and incubi will literally starve to death. The food the rest of us eat isn't enough to sustain them alone. Can they evolve enough to survive in the time that's left?

"Okay," David says, speaking for the first time. There's an expression of bullish determination on his face, though he's paler than usual. "This is… not ideal, but…" He trails off. "Sam, it's absolutely definite? The only way to stop the deterioration is by humans learning about us?"

The lucifer opens his mouth to answer, then stops and frowns. "Could you ask that again, please?"

David exchanges a look with Andrew, who sits up, his gaze on the lucifer. "Is the only way to stop the loss of our abilities to tell humans we exist?"

Lucifer Sam looks bemused. "No."

A murmur races around the room. "But you said," Imani starts, and David holds up a hand.

"So we don't have to tell humans we exist?" he asks, watching the lucifer intently.

"We don't."

"How do we get around that?" Noah demands. "Let them think they discovered magic on their own? They're still probably going to cause mass destruction." He winces. "Should I be saying 'we' instead of 'they'?"

"No," several voices declare.

"You're one of us," Andrew says firmly.

"Noah has a good point, though," David muses.

"Sam, will the issue be resolved if humans re-learn magic use without discovering anything about the community?"

The lucifer nods slowly, then looks over at Brandt and the king. "That seems like a pretty strong yes?"

"That's what I'm getting," Brandt confirms, and the king nods.

"Me too."

Relief rushes through me, but dissipates when Gideon says, "It's not enough. You give humans—all humans—magic, and they'll rip this world apart. We'll all be dead within decades, not centuries, and we may even be forced to come out of hiding to protect ourselves."

"Does it have to be all humans?" I ask before I can stop myself. It's the first time I've spoken to anyone other than Fabian—there's really no official need for me to be here, except I came with Fabian.

"Uh…" The lucifer looks taken aback. "…no."

"What does that mean?" David asks frustratedly. "Now would be a really good time for clear communication."

I decide to push ahead with my theory. "Humans outnumber us, right? So to achieve balance, not all humans would need to be using magic. Just an equivalent number to our population." I glance uncertainly at Brandt. I know him better than the lucifer and feel more comfortable looking at him. "Right?"

"Yes," Brandt agrees, smiling widely.

"That's an excellent point, uh… Rhys, isn't it?" the lucifer says.

"Rhys Griffiths, sir." I half raise my hand to wave,

then force myself to lower it. Now is not the time to be socially awkward.

"*Dr.* Griffiths," Fabian adds proudly. I feel my face getting hot, but it makes me all melty inside that he's boasting on my behalf.

"Rhys is responsible for the study that shows regular sexual activity improves metaphysical health," David explains, casting me a sideways smile.

"Gideon and I want to sign up for that," Lucifer Sam announces. "Especially now, because apparently that study is going to help us all rebuild our metaphysical muscles when the balance is restored."

"What?" Gideon demands. It would be a lot more intimidating if he wasn't staring at his boyfriend besottedly. How can a person go from batshit terrifying to this in just a few seconds?

The lucifer taps the side of his head and then looks to Brandt and the king. "That's what I got."

"Same," King Raðulfr agrees. "Once the balance is restored, we can work on reversing the damage."

David squints. "So the first step is to establish our population number... I'm assuming that includes the elves but not the dragons?"

The three leaders nod.

"Okay. Then we determine an equivalent number of humans that can learn magic without deciding to go on a rampage and destroy us all."

"Start with humans like me," Noah suggests. "People who are already part of the community. Spouses, parents, kids. We're already teaching some of them, so we'll just expand the program faster than planned."

"They would also be a good source to identify others

who can be trusted," Alistair points out. "They know what's at stake, have a vested interest in protecting the community. And they've proven themselves trustworthy, keeping our secret from their friends and families. They're not likely to give us away by nominating someone unsuitable."

"But accidents happen," Gideon argues. "A whole lot of what CSG does is contain accidental exposures. What if someone they think they can trust turns out to have a crazy grudge and uses their newfound magic on an ex or something?"

"That's what CSG is for," the lucifer reminds him. "We expand operations, add a human magic management department or something. This is within our scope."

The king and Brandt exchange glances. "The DEA would be interested in making human management an inter-government function," his majesty says. "We all live in this world with humans, and I imagine that both elves and dragons will intermarry with them eventually."

"Thank you," the lucifer says. "That sounds like an excellent idea. I think we can leave the arrangements to David and Caolan?"

There's agreement all around.

"That's a start," David says, "but we'll still be short some humans."

"What about Wiccans?" Noah asks. "They already dabble. What if we show them how to increase their use of magic? The main tenet of their religion is to do no harm, so they're a pretty safe bet."

"I like that idea."

Mine is not the only shocked face that turns to

Gideon. He *likes* something? Is that possible? Other than the lucifer, that is.

"We should stick to that theme," he continues. "People and groups that have made a commitment to being peaceful. There have to be *some*. Then we have a human who's already part of the community, like Noah, go in and show them how to use magic but make a big deal about how it has to be secret to prevent someone from misusing it."

"Not Noah," Noah says immediately. "Please not Noah."

"But you're such a good teacher," Andrew says wickedly. "Everyone says so."

"The ones that don't quit in despair, anyway," Alistair adds. "What? Don't all give me reproachful looks. Noah knows he's an asshole."

Noah nods. "It's something I've cultivated. Keeps the idiots away. Most of them, anyway."

I think I need to get out of here before I inadvertently show how appalled I am that these people are running our government. What was the magic *thinking*?

Although… they must be doing something right, since they put systems in place that actually led to the greatest issue we've ever faced being solved.

David takes the reins of conversation back. "Okay, we'll start with that and see where it gets us. At least we're taking steps, right? Fabian, you said some of the information that led you to this came from a paper written about human magic use?"

Silence.

I glance over at my boyfriend and see he's zoned right out. Percy sighs, Brandt chuckles, and I nudge him before anyone else can see the glazed look in his eyes.

Maybe they'll just think he's considering his answer instead of ignoring the whole conversation.

He starts when my elbow makes contact with his ribs. "What?"

David, eyes dancing with amusement, repeats the question.

"Yes. It was written by Achatius. I've been meaning to have it translated and send it over, but I got distracted."

"The DEA will take care of the translation," Caolan offers.

"Is there anything else that refers to human magic use?" David asks. "Anything we can mine for more information?"

"I'm sure there is." Fabian shrugs. "I can begin a search, if you like?"

"I'll help," Eerika adds. "Really, we should have done more than a cursory search to begin with."

"And Rhys can continue his research," David says with a note of finality. "It seems we'll be looking to expand it in the future."

"Of course," I manage, trying not to freak out at the idea that the study I designed is going to be what heals millennia of damage to our metaphysical health. If this wasn't a top-secret, let's-not-panic-people-by-telling-them-what's-happening thing, it would make me famous.

The meeting breaks up, with David promising that Noah will send notes to everyone—and Noah making a face about it—and as people start leaving the room, Brandt and Percy come to join us.

"Excellent work, you two," Percy says with a warm

smile. I instantly feel like I've just won an award. "You've saved the community."

"There's a lot of work ahead," I demur.

"But none of it could be done if we weren't so awesome," Fabian adds, and I nearly choke on my laugh.

"What were you thinking about?" Brandt asks. "It must have been important, if not even the fate of the world could keep your attention."

"It was very important," Fabian says solemnly. "I'm thinking of expanding my hoard to include nipple rings."

"You want to get your nipples pierced?" Sophie asks curiously as she joins us.

He shakes his head. "Oh, no. They're not for me."

Almost as one, their eyes turn to me.

"Hard pass. No, Fabian." I am *not* getting my nipples pierced just so he can put more rings on me.

He smiles confidently. "You don't need to decide right now. We have time. Like, *forever*."

Brandt claps his hands. "That's right, Kethe said you had big relationship news."

"It's complicated," Fabian says solemnly. "Rhys didn't realize I love him because he needed to hear me say it. He thought we were just dating casually. So I planned an epic night of romance." He pats my arm. "He knows now."

I'd be embarrassed about my private life being shared this way, but I've been around the dragons for half a year now. I know their ways. Privacy is an illusion.

"Was it really an epic night of romance?" Percy asks me, eyes twinkling. More than anyone else at Here Be

Dragons, he understands how interesting it can be to date a dragon.

"He pulled out all the stops, but he did it thinking about what I'd want. It was perfect." I smile at Fabian, trying not to look too sappy. In the past thirty hours, so much has changed. I no longer need to worry that this is going to end, and it's made such a difference.

"I did," he says proudly. "Though I still think the fireworks would have been epic. Oh, I forgot to update my posse."

Um… "Your what now?"

He pulls out his phone. "The humans who helped me yesterday at the store. They were all very impressed by how romantic I am. Except Deakin. He kept asking if we wanted a third." He stops typing and glances at me. "We don't, do we? I said no, but if you want to, he'd be a good choice."

I can't even… "It's definitely no," I say faintly, and this time it's Sophie who pats my arm.

"It'll be okay," she murmurs. "I'm so glad we have a sorcerer in the family now."

Somehow, that doesn't make me feel any better.

EPILOGUE

Fabian

THERE'S nothing quite so wonderful as skimming through the living archive while lying in bed beside my naked, ring-adorned boyfriend. He was reading through some of the latest data from his study, but his tablet now lies abandoned on the mattress beside him as he dozes lightly.

He's perfect.

Or he would be if he'd agree to pierce his nipples.

No, no, he's definitely perfect as he is. The nipples would just be a nice bonus. I've already begun searching out body jewelry and found the most lovely pair of ornate silver nipple rings with green stones that would perfectly match his eyes. There was a complementary piece designed for a Prince Albert, and all I've been able to think about since I saw it is how pretty Rhys's cock would look pierced.

I'm not going to mention cock piercing until after the nipples are done and he admits he likes them. Which he will, eventually. My Rhys is more adventurous than he thinks. Years of self-esteem issues have held him back, but the real him is starting to blossom.

But even if he never gets pierced, I'll still love him more than the breath in my body. I never even knew it was possible to feel this way. He's the only person I've ever met who I'll willingly and happily give up time in the archive to talk to. Because talking to Rhys is more important than the preservation of dragonkind's knowledge.

Plus, he's a lot hotter than my paperweight and gives better cuddles.

He stirs beside me and mumbles drowsily, "What are you doing?"

Stroking lightly over the velvety smooth skin covering his amazing biceps, I say, "Just working on the search for more human magic information. Go back to sleep." He's been working so hard lately and needs his rest.

Blinking sleepily, he peers up at me. "You were thinking about me."

Joy bursts through me. "I was. But then, I usually am."

He rolls on his side and snuggles closer. "I dreamed of you. We traveled with the Doctor in the Tardis. You looked great in his scarf."

Oooh, that could be a fun fantasy. We both like *Doctor Who*. But I'd want to take turns being the Doctor.

Though, does it even matter? The only important thing is the warm, beautiful sorcerer snuggling against me.

"I like when you dream of me."

"Our whole life together is a dream come true," he murmurs, eyes drifting closed again.

I can't argue with that. Sure, technically his species is slowly dying out, and the only way to save them is to break the most important rule they've lived by for the past nine thousand years and show humans how to use magic. And yes, humans as a species are notoriously volatile and destructive and may very well take this newly rediscovered ability and use it to launch a series of global conflicts that could wipe all of us out.

But those are just possibilities. Things could also work out well. And regardless of whether the world is destroyed by humans or saved by them, I get to live with Rhys. Get to love him and be loved by him. I get to adorn him with rings and spend lazy evenings in bed. If that's not a dream come true, then nothing is.

Thanks for reading the *The Dragon Experiment*! Want the bonus scene where Rhys gets his nipples pierced? Subscribe to my monthly newsletter: bit.ly/ LouisaMBonus and download it now!

The next (and final) book in the series is *Conspiracy of Dragons*, Steffen's book… and Wil's.

We talk spoilers in my Facebook Reader Group, RoMMance With Becca & Louisa.

For early access to chapters of my upcoming books, artwork, and other bonus material, check out my Patreon here: patreon.com/louisamasters

ALSO BY LOUISA MASTERS

Saddles & Suits

Alistair's Extraordinaries

Grave Situation

Elemental Men: The Complete Series

Style Me

Rebrand

Couture

Elf Magic

Wooing the Wiccan

Enticing the Elf

The Collective

Higher Demon

Demon Hunter

Demons-In-Law

Asher

Micah

Zachary

Franklin U

Mr. Romance

The Holigay Hookup *related novella

Batting Style

Ghostly Guardians

Spirited Situation

Vortex Conundrum

Conduit Crisis

Gateway Catastrophe

Here Be Dragons

Dragon Ever After

The Professor's Dragon

The Dragon Experiment

Conspiracy of Dragons

Hidden Species

Demons Do It Better

One Bite With A Vampire

Hijinks With A Hellhound

Sorcerers Always Satisfy

Hidden Species Box Set

Met His Match

<u>Charming Him</u>

<u>Offside Rules</u>

<u>A Christmas Chance (novella)</u>

<u>Between the Covers (M/F)</u>

Joy Universe

I've Got This

<u>Follow My Lead</u>

<u>In Your Hands</u>

<u>Take Us There</u>

Novellas

Fake It 'Til You Make It (permafree)

One Golden Night

O Hell, All Ye Shoppers

Out of the Office

After the Blaze

Blokes Down Under Novella Collection